for Demelza

The Constanţa Connection

Allan Brewer

ISBN: 978-1799243588

CONTENTS

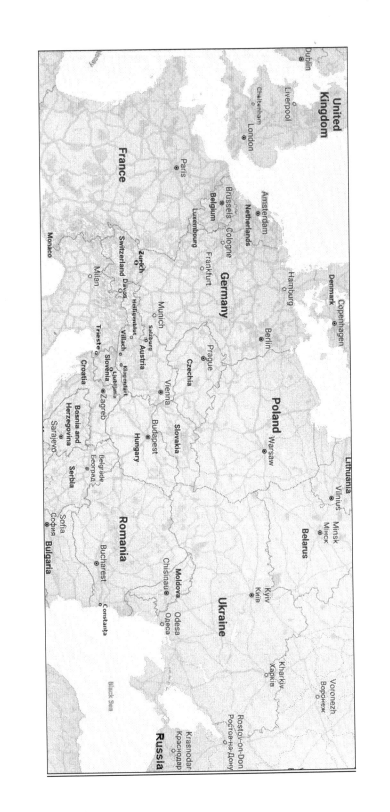

Chapter 1
Conflicting Destinies

Sergei lit another cigarette. It was one of his few pleasures. Though supposedly he was not allowed to smoke inside the chalet - he resented that. He opened the window a crack to blow the smoke out. It was freezing. Why should he care about smoking in the room? They would not be here much longer anyway, stuck in amongst these self-satisfied Western tourists and their damn ski gear. Dmitry was sleeping. It always seemed to be Sergei who got the uncomfortable jobs. Staying awake, watching out of a window for hours waiting to see their mark appear. They had tossed a coin to decide who should wait up - but Sergei had suspicions about Dmitry's coin tossing. Their intelligence boss had told them that it should be sometime during this night. Sergei had been watching for 5 hours now. To get a good view of the car he had to lean over from his seat, so he was cold and stiff, and on to his last pack of decent cigarettes. Next week he could get back to smuggling cigarettes across the Ukraine/Romanian border - good brands like St. George or Ronson - easy work, just driving, no tedious uncomfortable waiting and watching out of a window all night. This made good money, true, but risky if they got stopped by the police - back home, smuggling, he could pay off the police if he got stopped, and still turn a profit for the night. Yes, this damn boring, uncomfortable job was not worth the trouble. His rambling resentments were suddenly replaced by rapt attention to the car. Now the adrenaline was flowing. There she was, opening the boot to load her bag, at long last. Sergei stubbed out his cigarette on the windowsill in a final act of disrespect, and rushed to wake Dmitry, who was sleeping in his clothes ready for a quick start. It only took a minute or so. They were out of the door just as an unsuspecting, and otherwise preoccupied Betty was driving off, away from Heiligenblut.

Maxim Kuznetsov was controlling the operation from a hotel room in Constanţa, on the Romanian coast. He was looking out of his hotel room window at the marina below, where the yacht was all prepared to spirit the English woman away across the Black Sea. His agent in Paris had phoned to confirm that they were ready to furnish the substitute body and coffin as soon as he gave the order. This was an excellent scheme - the English intelligence service would not even be aware that they had lost a key scientist with vital secrets. At least, his organisation assumed she had big secrets - they had been tipped off that something special was happening in that annexe building to GCHQ. He had been patient for months, understanding her moves and intentions from monitoring her phone calls and messages, waiting to identify an opportunity. The attempt to isolate her from her employers, by getting her fired from GCHQ itself had failed - but in retrospect that just seemed to confirm how valuable she was to them - if they allowed her to carry on working there after breaking the rules on drugs. And now, finally knowing that she was to holiday in Austria, where she would be vulnerable to an intercept. But it was incredible luck that he then learned she was going to seek voluntary euthanasia in Zurich. That created the opportunity to disappear her without the English even knowing. And then yesterday she had booked the flight to Zurich. But now it all depended on his Romanian hirelings to get the intercept right. He wondered for a moment whether he should have brought in some more experienced and skilled agents. But the Romanians had done a previous job for him without any problem; there was no point in exposing valuable agents to risk unless it was absolutely necessary.

It was almost dawn - he glanced at the laptop screen again. Ah, the tracked phone had now been turned off, but the car-tracker was showing movement out of Heiligenblut. The final pieces were falling into place. He felt a flash of concern whether the Romanians would be on to it - should he phone them to make sure? No, better not to disturb them at this point - they should have seen the car preparing to leave even before Maxim could detect it anyway. He took a deep breath and went to fix some breakfast - the Romanians had been instructed to phone confirmation to him as soon as they had secured the intercept.

Betty was driving extra carefully, hoping that she would not experience any involuntary jerks on the road to Salzburg. It had happened to her only four times in the last five days, and, as a mathematician, she could not help but figure that gave her over 80% chance of getting the 2.5 hours to the airport without an incident.

It would be her last ever drive. Then, her last ever plane flight. She had decided to walk out on her life, rather than live on in a compromised way. That had always been her plan - ever since she was diagnosed with the gene. It was clear - her thoughts were always clear. Except suddenly it was all feeling surreal - choosing to die was not a straightforward, clear choice. Suddenly the clarity was gone and the tears started to come. She pulled over in a lay-by and let the sobs come, better to let the sadness pass through her now than try to suppress it for the next two hours. She doubled over the steering wheel feeling the waves of regret welling up from deep in her belly, ending as pain in her throat as she let out some loud howls. She knew how to cry - she even did that well, but this was more primal, and not so quick to pass.

A flash of lights caught her eye over to the right, and momentarily distracted, she looked over, shocked to see a vehicle toppling over the barrier at the hairpin bend some way back. It then plunged down the side of the mountain onto a lane that was just a little way to her right. Her hand came up to her mouth as she gasped in horror at the sight. An urgent wave of shock and concern washed away her previous self-absorbed feelings. Since the lane was narrow and snowy, she left the car in the lay-by and took to the lane on foot. It led down to a chalet. A light went on in a downstairs window as she approached - the owner woken by the sound of the crash. The vehicle, a black van, had somersaulted down the slope and landed right-way-up in the snow to the side of the chalet, its windows broken and its bodywork dented and deformed, squatting, strangely silent. Urgency pushed Betty to try to run the last 50 metres to the van but the snow was too deep and instead, she had to make large, slow sensible strides to cover the ground as fast as she could. Finally arriving at the van, she yanked at the driver-side door, but it had jammed in the crash. The window, though, was shattered, so she banged away the fragmented glass with her gloved hand. The driver, she saw, was slumped sideways across the steering wheel. Betty felt his neck for a pulse. His face was bloody and there was a strange black line running up the side of his face. He had no pulse. But there was a moaning sound from a man in the passenger seat. Betty worked her way around the van through the thick snow to reach the other door. It swung open all too easily and the bleeding passenger slid sideways off the seat, his head landing on the snow, his feet still in the van, so that he was upside down. He was writhing in agony and trying to talk, but it was unintelligible, not so much because the language was foreign, but because the muscles of his mouth did not seem to be working properly. He also had a black line running up one side of his

3

face, Betty now noticed, as he tried in vain to right himself.

At that moment a sturdy man came stomping out of the chalet shouting in German "*Was zur Hölle ist hier passiert?*" (What the hell has happened here?) He had a torch in one hand and his phone in the other, and was already calling the emergency services. Betty explained in German, as best she could, what little she knew so far. As the injured passenger struggled, the fact that he was upside down caused the contents of his trouser pocket to start spilling out onto the snow - a packet of cigarettes, money... Reflexively Betty reached down to gather the items and found her hand on a gun. For a second it ran through her mind that they might be police officers, though there was no such indication from their clothing. But then, with the injured man writhing about, safety considerations prevailed, and she quickly lifted the gun and offered it, grip forward, to the man from the chalet. "*Gewehr!!*" (Gun!) he exclaimed in alarm taking a step back, and refusing to accept it. She slipped it into her own pocket instead. He shone his torch directly down onto the injured passenger, and Betty saw that amongst the other things spilling from his pocket was a photograph. As she again bent over to gather up the items spilling out, she realised with astonishment, as the torchlight played there, that it was a photograph of herself. For a few seconds a surreal feeling cut in again, and she wondered in quick succession whether perhaps she was dreaming or already dead - a photo of herself made absolutely no sense in this setting. But in Betty's sharp mind, the realisation slammed home pretty quickly that a gun and photo of her, in a vehicle following her, added up to a serious menace to her personally. Apparently, by providence, her immediate danger had been averted, but it may have been only partially or temporarily deferred. She placed the contents of the man's pocket on the floor of the van, but slipped the incongruous photo into her own pocket.

The man from the chalet was now wrenching at the side door of the van, to see if there were any other casualties inside. The door protested with an ugly grinding sound as it jammed halfway open. There was only a jumble of blankets and luggage inside. The man from the chalet tugged at the blankets and gently put a bundle underneath the head of the injured passenger. Betty pulled out another blanket, revealing some broken glass and a strange smell - ether, she wondered. She laid the blanket over the injured man. The potential scenario was now unfolding in detail in her mind - she knew what information they would have wanted from her - this was extremely serious. But how had they known that she was party to invaluable technological knowledge, to the i-vector theory? And how had they known to find her, on *this* road, at *this* time?

She straightened and told the chalet man, "*Ich muss zum Flughafen kommen.*" (I must get to the airport.) He shrugged and nodded, obviously not relishing having to shoulder the responsibility on his own, but Betty had already realised she owed absolutely no obligation to this injured man, and now needed to consider her own safety as a priority. She took a last careful look at the faces of the two in the van, noticing that the driver had the strange thick black line up *this* side of his face as well as the other, just in front of his ears, although the passenger only had a black line up one side. It didn't seem to make sense, but stirred at something in her subconscious.

She strode off quickly back up the lane to her car, regretting that her legs were now wet and cold from the depth of the snow above her boots. It was just beginning to get light. Her foremost thought was to drive as fast as possible to the airport to be safer in the crowds and civilisation of the city. But a few paces from the car the realisation hit her - George was still sleeping back at the chalet in Heiligenblut, and he might also be in danger. True, he did not have the technical knowledge that the abductors were after, but that would not protect him if the abductors did not realise that. She would have to go back. No, she could phone UK security from here, now, they would look after George. But could they get to him in time? She should phone UK security anyway, now. She had turned her phone off when she had left the chalet because she wanted to avoid having to deal with an emotionally difficult call from George, when he realised that she was gone. She took out her phone, but stopped again. No one had known that she would take this road now, except for a single phone message she had made to the airline yesterday. Her phone calls were maybe... probably, being monitored. She cursed. It was difficult to make correct decisions when you did not know all the variables accurately. She took a deep breath. Weigh the probabilities. She paused for a moment. Best to get back to Heiligenblut, find a different phone to talk to UK security. And unknown to the adversary, she also had a gun in her pocket. Ha! Not that she knew how to use it - but she was technically adept - she could work that out. She turned the car around and headed back to Heiligenblut.

Motivation had now flooded out her earlier feelings - indeed, when she briefly thought about it, she now found it difficult to connect with the reasons for her journey to end her life. But that could all be sorted out afterwards. What to tell George? Hopefully he was still asleep; hopefully he had not found the 'goodbye' letter?

She was relieved to get the few minutes drive back to

Heiligenblut without any incident. She parked the car in the same spot as before. It was a little after 6:15 am. Damn, she had left behind her key-card for the front door of the chalet, not thinking she would need it again. She tried the door - it was locked. And the church where she played the piano would also still be locked. She would have to wait in the car until the chalet cook arrived to fix breakfasts - was she a sitting duck in the car? How many other hostile agents might be here? She sat down low in the driver seat of the car, anxiously looking around and keeping an eye on the rear-view and wing mirrors, whilst furtively checking out the gun in her lap. It was not obvious how it worked - she could make a guess at the safety catch, but she did not know if it was even loaded. Still, it could buy her time in an emergency just by revealing it - judging by the reaction of the man from the chalet - "*Gewehr!*" She laughed gently, remembering the look on his face. She hadn't even meant to walk away with the gun, but it certainly gave a feeling of power, of reassurance. She checked the mirrors again. Anyway, later she could get details about the gun from the internet, or phone Harriet, a military colleague back at GCHQ, for advice. Someone was trudging up the snowy slope on the other side. Bundled up unrecognisably, but who wouldn't be on this cold morning? Betty gently slipped the key back in the ignition ready for a quick getaway if necessary, and closed her hand on the gun, waiting, as the figure got nearer. He walked past, appearing not to notice her sitting in the car. She maintained her readiness, watching intently in the rear-view mirror, until he finally walked into a chalet entrance further up the hill. She took a long breath, realising that her heart had been pounding.

She took another look at the handgun she was holding. It had a brown handgrip with a small five-pointed star design engraved on it. That should make it easy to identify, she considered. The brown handgrip and the star brought back memories of the toy cowboy gun her brother had played with as a small boy, though this gun was clearly a pistol rather than a revolver. He had gone through a phase of running around with his friends; pretending to fire at each other, recreating a cowboy western adventure. She had been rather disdainful of those games of the younger boys, and had never wanted to join in, but the memory brought back a feeling of fondness for her brother and his enthusiasm.

Her attention returned to the gun. But this gun did not have a belly like a revolver - it seemed to be the type of gun into which you loaded a magazine of cartridges, through the heel of the grip. She glanced in the mirrors and looked ahead again - Nothing. Back to the gun. There was a small up/down catch on the left-hand side of the gun -

6

presumably the safety catch - but was up, or down, safe? Fascinating. Betty, as a scientist, found her interest being naturally drawn toward the mechanism of the handgun; and she could begin to understand why military types like Harriet were interested in weaponry. Another quick glance around. Someone else was trudging up the snowy hill. Betty tensed again. But this time she recognised the blue and red coloured logo of the holiday company staff. Ah, the chalet cook for the breakfasts, at last. Betty waited until she was close, then stepped out of the car.

"Hi Hannah, I got myself locked out." Hannah clearly recognised her, and let them both in through the front door. The staff were mostly student age, working a season here, enthusiastic and eager to please, no reason to be suspicious of anything. "Hey Hannah, would you mind lending me your phone for 10 minutes - I need to make a call and my phone is very low on battery?" Betty hated having to lie - but it was only a small white one, in a good cause, she considered.

Betty retreated to the corner of the empty lounge with Hannah's phone, briefly turned her own phone back on, and copied the GCHQ UK security number out of it. She then turned it off again and buried it under a cushion in case it was bugged. It would be even earlier, by an hour, in the UK, but security staffed the place round the clock, and indeed she was not kept waiting.

"Hello, this is Betty Gosmore, from project BH9, top security. I am on holiday in Austria and there has been a failed attempt to kidnap me. I need advice and help urgently." Betty was concise and clear as always, packing the most relevant information into minimal sentences. The security officer on the other end, however, was used to dealing with local issues and was immediately out of his depth. After asking Betty to repeat some of the details, his protocols were clear enough to him that he knew he had to pass this on to MI5 immediately, and he told Betty to wait for a call back from them. There was a painful wait as the information was passed up the chain to duty officers, and finally to someone with authority. Betty waited tensely as Hannah made a few bustling appearances, kitting out the table with the usual inviting array of breakfast food. Betty was also painfully aware that George would be awake soon, and she desperately wanted to remove the 'goodbye' letter before he saw it, otherwise there would be emotional complications added to an already scary situation. Writing and leaving that letter to George now seemed like a memory from a different world. Finally, someone called Tom Wheatley rang her back on Hannah's phone. Although he sounded as if he had just been woken up, his voice nevertheless conveyed reliability and clarity along with urgency.

"So, I understand I am speaking to Betty Gosmore, top secret clearance, GCHQ, on holiday in Austria, and there has been a kidnap attempt, is that correct?"

"Yes." The reassuring depth in his voice, finally satisfying her undeclared need for emotional support, found Betty giving a couple of sobs of relief.

"OK, tell me the basic details of what happened," he requested gently.

"I set off to drive from the ski resort to the airport, Salzburg, and about 10 minutes into the journey, a van came off the road at a hairpin bend behind me and crashed down the hill. I rushed over to where the van had landed, out of concern - there were two men, one was dead, the other badly injured, and he had a gun."

"OK, but why did you think they were out to kidnap you?" asked Wheatley failing to see any connection.

"Oh, well he had a photo of *me* in his pocket," explained Betty.

"But how could you possibly know that - do you mean you went through his pockets?" Wheatley sounded just slightly sceptical.

"No, no, he fell out sideways when I opened the door, and stuff started sliding out of his pocket. I was just trying to be helpful by gathering the things up. Oh, and there was an organic smell of ether or chloroform or something from a broken bottle in the back of the van."

"Was the injured man aggressive toward you?"

"No, no, he was very badly injured - delirious, and unable to move much." Betty shuddered slightly at the uncomfortable memory.

"OK Betty, well it sounds like we got very lucky this morning then. Firstly, lucky that they crashed, and secondly, even more fortunate that, because you attended the crash, we found out about the plot. So where are you now?"

"Back in Heiligenblut, the ski resort."

"But why didn't you just drive on to the airport?" questioned Wheatley.

"Oh, well, I have a colleague with me here, I was concerned for his safety too. So I came back. But also to borrow a phone to get in touch with you guys - I'm assuming my own phone may be hacked - how else could they have known my plans?" Betty tested her conclusion against Wheatley's experience.

"Yes, you may well be right, very sensible. What is your colleague's name?"

"He is George Tremaine. So, what should we do now? Can you get protection to us, or should we drive to the airport?" Betty felt she needed authoritative advice.

"Right... well, it would be some hours before I could get an agent to you. My advice is that you should both turn your phones off in case they are being tracked, wrap them in aluminium foil if you can, in case they contain a bug with its own power supply - the aluminium foil will block any signal - and then drive to the airport as soon as you can. You should be relatively safe once you reach the city. It is unlikely the kidnappers would have a backup team. And in any case, they may not yet know what has happened to their personnel. They almost certainly do not know where you are now, or what you intend to do. So, we need to get you out of the area whilst we still have those advantages, and before they can regroup. Also, take this borrowed phone with you so that we can keep in touch, and I can get some more details from you. Obviously, we will start working this end to find out exactly how your security has been breached - I'm really sorry you've had this frightening experience, Betty. Which UK airport are you flying into? - I'll meet you there."

"Oh, OK, well, Bristol is nearest to home, if we can get a flight, I *was* booked to Zurich, but... not now." Betty realised that what she really wanted, more than anything else was to get home as soon as possible. Her previous rational state, that had allowed her to make the emotionally difficult decision to go to Zurich, had now been rattled by events.

"Right," acknowledged Wheatley. "Well, let me know the UK flight when you check in at Salzburg airport, and I will try to meet you when you land."

"OK, thanks, I'll go and tell George now... bye." Betty took a deep breath - at least now, she had a clear plan.

Hannah was back in the room, setting out the cutlery on the dining table. "Would you like me to fix you breakfast now?" she offered with a great big smile, "The other guests will be down soon, if they're not too hung over from the New Year celebrations last night!"

"Oh, thanks, but no, Hannah. We have got to leave this morning and I need to get the packing done. But could you give me a sheet of

9

aluminium foil from the kitchen, please? And thanks so much for lending me your phone." She handed the phone back to Hannah. Despite what Tom Wheatley had advised, she felt that she couldn't take Hannah's phone, or even offer to buy it. Poor Hannah would have no way of buying another in this small ski resort. Hannah emerged from the kitchen again with a roll of aluminium foil from which Betty tore off a large sheet. "Actually, you know what. Yes, Hannah, I *would* love a full breakfast, but wait till I come back down with George in a few minutes."

Betty, feeling a little more confident after the conversation with Wheatley, retrieved her own phone from under the cushion where she had muffled it. Then she made her way upstairs to their room. Opening the door gingerly, she was relieved to find George was still in bed asleep. She quickly retrieved the potentially confusing and complicating 'goodbye' letter from next to her pillow, and folded it into one of her pockets. She wanted to change her leggings, which, though her legs were no longer cold, were still wet from the deep snow. But all her clothes were packed, in a case in the car. Postponing that until later, she sat on the bed lightly next to George and began to rouse him gently. "George, wake up honey, you need to wake up now."

"Umm… Oh good morning sweetheart," he yawned. They embraced. "Uh? you're all wet, are you back from the church already? What's the time?" he muttered.

"Listen, George, this is really important. There was an attempt to kidnap me. I'm fine - don't worry, but we need to leave here as soon as we can. For our safety." George sat straight upright in bed, his eyes wide and brow furrowed. At that exact moment, George's alarm went off, startling them both. George took a deep breath. "What happened, was this on the way to the church? You're not joking are you?"

She squeezed his hand in assurance, and leaned over to silence the alarm. "Oh, and we need to turn our phones off - there's a good chance that they are hacked or bugged and we might be tracked. I will fill you in on all the details on the way. I have spoken with MI5 on the phone, and they are advising us to get on the road to the airport as soon as possible, so let's pack your stuff, grab some breakfast and go." She strode to the closet, got George's bag out and started throwing in the clothes that she could see.

"It's OK, I'll do that, you get yours packed." He swung out of bed.

"Mine are already in the car," stated Betty.

"What? How?" George was puzzled.

"Look, it's complicated. Please save the questions until later. Let's get ourselves safe first. I promise I'll answer all your questions properly then." She said this decisively so that George would comply, though inside he was struggling to comprehend what was going on, and finding it hard to focus on the packing.

"I'm going downstairs," she continued, "and I'll order us a couple of full breakfasts - you come down in a few minutes when you've finished packing. But don't say anything to the others at breakfast - we need to keep our situation as discreet as possible." Betty was trying to avoid explanation, at least until she had the space to talk properly with George. Although he would understand the security and the events that happened on the road easily enough, the fact that she was driving away to the airport would require a complete explanation of her illness and decision, and indeed of the status of their relationship. She regretted the unfortunate convolution of the two otherwise-unrelated chains of events, making everything potentially so much more difficult.

George finished packing his case and freshened himself up. He could sense the danger that they would be in if some hostile state had somehow got wind of the valuable nature of their knowledge about the i-vector system, but Betty was clearly hiding something else from him and was unwilling as yet, to explain fully. However, he trusted her well enough to allow her to do that, without pushing her for answers. When he got down to the dining room there were a couple of other guests chatting with Betty about the weather and piste-route plans for the day, and Hannah was serving up plates of hot breakfast with her customary big smile. He sat down beside Betty with a quick hug. "All done," he whispered. She smiled and touched his arm reassuringly and appreciatively.

Ten minutes or so later, they were loading George's case into the car ready to set out. "Do you mind doing the driving please?" requested Betty.

"Sure," replied George obligingly, as he eyed the state of the road by the chalet with a little apprehension - it had a liberal covering of snow, mowed into ruts by the previous day's traffic. He started the car and pulled out gently, getting the feel of the tyres on the snow. "So now you can explain to me exactly what happened?"

Betty inhaled deeply, thinking about how to organise her

explanation. "Look, George," she began, "there are two *separate* issues that I need to explain to you. The first is that I was driving to the airport a couple of hours ago - but I would like to defer explaining to you *why* I was doing that, until we can sit down together properly."

George felt his heart sink. "What... you were leaving?" he asked plaintively and incredulously.

"No, not like that," Betty leaned across and put her hands affectionately on his shoulder, "I wasn't leaving you, or because of you... it's to do with my health. But that's why I want to explain it later, it's... complicated. Anyway, please just take it as given that I was driving to the airport," she continued quickly, trying to shut down further conversation on that subject. "And then, after a few miles, I stopped by the side of the road because I was feeling, well, a bit emotionally upset about leaving. And then, it was still quite dark at that time, I noticed a flashing of lights above and to my side, and I saw it was a van, crashing over the barrier at the hairpin bend, about a half a mile behind where I had got to. It kind of somersaulted down the mountainside, its headlights arcing through the snow and trees, and finished up just down a lane, fairly close to where I had stopped. I was horrified and concerned of course, so I got out and went down the lane to see if I could help the people in the van. There was a local man too, came out of a chalet close by to help - he phoned the emergency services."

George was listening intently, talk of a van crashing had subconsciously motivated him to slow a little, even though the surface of the local road was rather easier than it had been back by the chalet.

"So," she continued, "there were two guys in the van, the driver was already dead, and the other was very badly injured - he kind of tumbled half out of the van when I opened the door, and things were falling out of his pocket onto the snow. I tried to gather them up and put them on the van floor, but that's when I found he had a gun."

George shot a look of sudden concern over at Betty.

"It's OK, I took the gun away - he was in no fit state to be able to use it anyway. But then, when the Austrian local man shone his torch down on the injured guy, I realised that the things falling out of his pocket included a photo of me - he had a photo of *me*, George, in his pocket." Betty gave a couple of short sobs, remembering the enormity of her realisation. "They must have been following me, intending to kidnap me, George."

George frowned. "Wait a minute Betty, are you sure it was a

12

photo of you? - it's easy to mistake something like that in half-light?" he cautioned.

"Yes - I'm certain." Betty put her hand into her pocket and pulled out the photo. She looked at it briefly for the first time since pocketing it - in truth, George's comment had instantiated a transient doubt in her mind, but it was quickly dispelled. She held it up in front of George's face so that he could look at it without taking his eyes far from the road.

"Well, yes... it's a photo of you all right," he confirmed. "But are you sure it came from the van? - It didn't perhaps fall out of your own pocket or something?" he asked, still wary of accepting the significance of the coincidence.

"Yes, of course I'm sure it didn't," she retorted a little crossly. She looked at the photo more closely. "It's not one of *my* photos - I don't even recognise where it's taken. And I don't carry around photos of me - why would I?"

George's confusion suddenly made his mind snap back to the time Betty had played an elaborate hoax on him by a riverside, even hiring an actor to hammer the credibility home. He was silent for a moment, unsure whether to question her sincerity, as she clearly seemed rattled by her experience - though of course, she was more than capable of acting that part if she wanted to. Then there was her lack of an explanation for why she was driving away in the first place; surely, she would have constructed a full story if she was conducting a hoax - or might that be a double-bluff?

"Oh, God." Betty had also been silent for a minute and brought her hand up to her throat. "This is the hairpin here - please drive carefully George, in case there is some ice on the road... or something."

George slowed the car to even more of a crawl than he normally would for a hairpin. Certainly, the low crash barrier was badly distorted and broken at the bend by something that had hit it. Perhaps, he wondered, Betty had heard about a crash earlier and had brought him out here to wind him up with the story?

George thought he would push for more information. "So, apart from the photo, was there anything else that made you think they were out to kidnap you?" he asked, trying not to betray his scepticism.

Betty seemed absorbed, and not paying full attention to his motivation. "Well, it all seemed so surreal, seeing that photo - up to that point I had just assumed they were unlucky victims of an accident. Then it all suddenly added up - a van not far behind me, a photo of me, a gun - that was when I realised. Oh, and then the Austrian guy yanked the side door half-open, there were lots of blankets so we pulled them out to make the injured guy more comfortable, and there was a strong smell of something volatile - I think it might have been ether - and bits of broken bottle. Betty shuddered again at the remembrance. So, then I just decided to get the hell out of there. Their faces were weird too - they had black lines down them - that made no sense. So I left. I thought of going straight on to Salzburg airport, but as I thought about it, I realised that you might be a target too, so I went back to Heiligenblut, and it was going to be quicker to borrow a phone there - I needed to let security know, and I didn't want to use my own phone. The only way they could have known I would be on that road at that time was if they had obtained access to my calls of yesterday. I borrowed Hannah's phone at the chalet and got put through to MI5 - damn I forgot to write down his phone number - he told me to keep Hannah's phone but I couldn't do that to her. We can buy a new phone when we get to Salzburg..." She tailed off at that point, as, two turns after the hairpin, there was an assortment of vehicles blocking the road. A couple of police cars were positioned to hold back any traffic, whilst a flatbed recovery truck was manoeuvring into position to winch the crashed van out of the lane.

"Oh, no," muttered Betty anxiously.

"It's OK," George said soothingly, "we'll be on our way again as soon as they shift the wreck."

"Yes, I just don't like being here again," Betty sounded anxious. "We need to get to the airport."

George pulled up behind the police car in response to the police officer's signal. George lowered his window as the officer strolled up. He looked in. "Engleesh?"

George nodded, "Ja."

"Please, for a few minutes you wait. We load a vehicle."

"OK, thank you," George replied compliantly.

George left the engine running to keep the interior heater working, but settled back in his seat. He looked over to Betty. He was still unsure whether to believe her whole story, but she was looking very nervous. A sturdy man emerged from the lane in conversation with another couple of police officers. The man gestured up the side of the mountain whence the van had crashed, and then gestured toward the road, and shrugged. He looked briefly over at the car in which George and Betty were sitting and then turned back to the truck. Betty slid down into her seat, not wanting to be noticed, but it was too late - he did a double-take, then grabbed one of the police officers by the arm, and pointed to the car, saying something. They both strode over to Betty's side of the car. "Ja, das ist sie. Ich bin mir sicher." (Yes, that is her, I'm sure of it.) The police officer bent down and gestured to Betty to step out of the car.

"Were you here earlier, madam, just after the crash?" Suddenly the reality and truth of Betty's story hit home to George with a jolt. He opened his door and also stepped out.

"Yes, that was me," she had already calculated it was pointless trying to deny it. "Hello again," she smiled at the sturdy man from the chalet, but he did not respond.

"I would like to ask you a few questions, madam."

Betty nodded. "Of course." She had snapped out of her anxiety to act calm and cooperative.

"Did you see how the accident happened?" asked the officer.

"No, I only saw the van coming over the edge from up there and crashing down onto the lane over there." She pointed.

"So where were you exactly?" the officer continued.

"About there." She pointed again, this time onto the road close by.

There was a graunching sound from the truck up ahead, as the winch strained against the resistance of the wrecked van.

"You were in your car, driving?" asked the officer

"Yes."

"And you were with her also, sir?" the officer addressed George.

"No," replied George. Betty shook her head.

"So where were you, sir?" the officer persisted.

"I was still asleep back in Heiligenblut," supplied George.

There was the sound of broken glass scattering as one of the crashed van's windows gave up struggling to retain its integrity.

The police officer took out a notepad and jotted down

something.

"Wait please."

He walked over to the other police officers who were idly observing the winching and had a short conversation with them.

Two of the officers came back over with him.

The more senior officer, an inspector, now took up the questioning.

"To where were you driving earlier, madam?" queried the Inspector.

"To Salzburg airport," stated Betty.

"But here you are, more than two hours later, driving in the same direction? How is this?" The naturally suspicious nature of the Inspector had been piqued.

Betty sighed. "I went back to Heiligenblut to collect my friend here. I was distressed by the accident - I wanted him with me."

A metallic bang announced the arrival of the front of the crashed van onto the flatbed.

"So, did you come here on holiday together?" the Inspector persisted, unfazed by the disturbing sounds behind him.

"Yes."

"Then why were you leaving without him?" The inspector was obviously suspicious.

Betty's voice betrayed growing irritation. "For personal reasons," she replied curtly.

The officer furrowed his brow quizzically but did not pursue that answer further.

"And did you see or notice anything unusual at the hairpin bend when you drove through earlier?"

"No," replied Betty flatly.

"It is surprising that you were so close - were you involved in the crash in any way?" proffered the Inspector.

"No, I was already down here when it happened, as I told your colleague," Betty replied firmly.

The inspector gestured to one of the officers who walked slowly round their car, looking for any signs that it had been in a collision. He completed the cursory tour and shook his head to the Inspector.

"Did you know these men in the crashed van - had you seen either of them before - after all it is likely they were also staying in Heiligenblut, is it not?" the Inspector continued.

"No, I don't recall having seen either of them before," stated Betty.

"And you sir?" He turned to George. "Had you seen either of them before?"

George shrugged. "I don't know because I wasn't at the crash scene."

The Inspector nodded courteously - he had laid the trap and had half been expecting George to contradict his own story by unthinkingly, and thoughtlessly, stating that he did not recognise the men. The Inspector thought for a moment. There was a sound of chains being thrown across the flatbed truck as the van was finally being secured into position.

"You see, the problem I have is that there are some odd circumstances to the crash - the paramedics have reported unexplained injuries - we will know better after the autopsy. Do you mind if we search your car?"

"By all means." Betty gestured her palm toward the car.

The officers made short work of sifting through the contents of Betty and George's two bags in the boot, and checking inside the car and the glove compartment without finding anything significant.

"And your persons please?" The officer gestured for them to raise their arms for a pat-down body search. George noticed a flash of concern on Betty's face that he did not understand. It took the female officer only a few seconds to discover the gun lying in Betty's pocket. It was carefully removed and placed into a plastic evidence bag and handed to the Inspector. He looked at it carefully, clearly surprised. "A Makarov - now what is an English lady on holiday doing with a loaded Soviet pistol?" He skilfully clicked the heel of the pistol and unloaded the cartridge of rounds, whilst it was still inside the plastic bag.

"But it's not illegal to carry a firearm in Austria, is it?" responded Betty flatly.

"Hmm, no, in principle," replied the Inspector, "have you

registered it?"

But, at that point, the stout Austrian man from the chalet, who had been watching the scene unfold from a few paces away, decided to intervene.

"Sie nahm es von dem verletzten mann," (She took it from the injured man) he stated, pointing at the gun.

Betty didn't wait for the inspector's question. "Yes, it fell out of the injured man's pocket as he was writhing - I thought it was safer to get it out of the way. I tried to pass it to this Austrian gentleman from the chalet, she gestured toward him, but he shied away from taking it, so I just slipped it into my own pocket. I was just trying to keep us all safe - I wasn't trying to *steal* it."

The inspector looked back to the stout Austrian man questioningly for his version of events. "Ja," he shrugged in resignation, "Ja, ja, was auch immer, ich kann nicht erwartet werden, sich inmitten dieses ganzen Chaos um eine Waffe zu kümmern." (Yes, yes, whatever, I can't be expected to look after a gun in the middle of all this mayhem.)

The Inspector thought for a moment. "We are going to have to take you both back to Regional Police Headquarters in Villach to get full statements," he concluded.

"Please, no," protested Betty, with tears suddenly in her eyes, "I have to get to the airport and get back home."

"No, I am sorry, the inspector insisted, you removed a weapon from the scene, that alone justifies a full statement, and I need to interview you properly, not out here in the cold. Don't worry about your car, one of my officers will drive it to headquarters at Villach."

And with that, Betty was escorted to one police car and George to another.

Chapter 2
The Blizzard

Kuznetsov had grown increasingly agitated. He felt he had been very patient whilst having breakfast, waiting for that phone call from the Romanians to say they had intercepted and secured the English woman. It should have been simplicity itself - he had spoon-fed them the arrangements. It would be one of his most successful missions. But no call came. At length, he went back to his laptop to see where on the road the woman's car was. Just a few miles out of Heiligenblut! But he was certain he had seen the tracker moving out an hour ago. So had the Romanians trashed her car and left it there? He had told them to be careful so that they could drive it back to the hire company at the airport. That was an essential part of the plan so that the English security people would have no idea she had been abducted. Is that why they had not phoned? - they had trashed her car and were afraid to tell him? He decided to phone the Romanians to check what had been happening - no answer. That was very odd - Dmitry always answered the phone to him. He banged his fist on the table, and then paced around the room angrily. It was intolerable not knowing what was happening. A few minutes later, he phoned Dmitry again.

"Guten Tag?" a German voice answered uncertainly.

Kuznetsov was unprepared for that, and there was a short silence. But he quickly recovered his composure. "Ah, Guten Tag, who is this, please? I have phoned my nephew's number?"

Another short pause. "Ah, sir, I am sorry to tell you that the man carrying this phone has been involved in a traffic accident. I am a paramedic - we are taking the two men from the vehicle to the hospital at Klagenfurt.

"Oh mein Gott, how badly hurt are they?"

"Ah, well sir, if you phone the hospital in a couple of hours they will be able to give you an update."

"But how are they now? Are they conscious? Do they have serious injuries?"

"Well, sir, to be honest with you, it does not look good for either of them. I am sorry sir."

"Wah... was there another vehicle involved?"

"Not to my knowledge sir, their van went over the crash barrier at a hairpin near Heiligenblut. We are not attending the occupants of any other vehicle. It would be helpful, sir, if you could give us the names of these men, and contact details for their next of kin?"

"Mein Gott, mein Gott. No... no, I can't do that right now." Kuznetsov rang off.

"The fools, the damned stupid idiots," he shouted in rage. He flung the phone at the wall. "How the hell could they mess up something so simple? And so important." He kicked the armchair, but then sank into it, his hands over his head, a mixture of anger and disappointment churning through his head. After a while, he recovered his composure. He would need to follow routine procedure and ditch that phone - he wanted to leave no trace of a link between himself and the Romanians. He picked it up from the floor - its impact with the wall had cracked the screen - and that somehow improved his mood slightly. He turned it off and threw it in the trash-bin. He took out a new phone from his small stock in a cupboard and loaded his important numbers into it. He checked the laptop again. The tracker showed that her car was indeed progressing toward the Salzburg road. Damn, there was no way she could be intercepted now - in a couple of hours she would be at the airport. His mood was black. He downed a couple of whiskeys, and settled at the table, watching the small flashing red dot on the map on his screen, edging its way belligerently, and inevitably toward Salzburg. Or was it? He put the whiskey glass down. The red dot seemed to have departed from its inevitable route - it had turned off the Salzburg road and was heading southeast. Why, and where was she heading? Kuznetsov's mood began to lift - there might be hope yet. His eyes were riveted upon the red dot inching forward at an unbearably slow pace. He spent the next hour pacing the room and thinking, interspersed with sips of whiskey and checking the progress of the tracker.

At length, the red dot became stationary over the town of Villach. It was time for Kuznetsov to make a decision. Without the Romanians to do the dirty work, he would have to pull his valuable agents down from Vienna. He looked on the map - a three and a half hour drive from Vienna to Villach - it was feasible. He judged that the potential payoff was worth the small risk of exposing the men, and phoned Jakob.

"Listen Jakob, this is Kuznetsov, I have some action for you. We have a tracker on the car of an Englishwoman who is a highly valuable intelligence target. She is in Villach. I want you and Felix to drive down there now and execute an abduction. Bring her to me in Constanța - I have the rest already organised."

Jakob had listened carefully. "We cannot get there today, Maxim, there are blizzards blocking the roads to the south of Austria."

"Ah, blizzards - that might explain a lot." Kuznetsov was apt to weave the snippets of information he gleaned into a coherent story, sometimes correct, sometimes not. So, maybe the Romanians had run afoul of a blizzard, yes, and the Englishwoman had driven to Villach because the road to Salzburg was too treacherous.

"But listen Maxim," Jakob continued, "the blizzards are forecast to cease tonight so the roads should be cleared by morning. We can drive down then. The target is unlikely to be able to leave Villach before morning anyway. Send us, now, the tracker identity code, and photos of the target, and we will gather the essentials and do the preparation."

"Excellent Jakob, I know I can rely on you. Make the abduction as 'quiet' as possible - afterwards, the preference would be to return her hire-car to an airport so as to leave the track cold."

"Understood Maxim. Let us have the details and I will contact you again when we are in position."

*   *   *

The journey time to Villach, in the police cars, was an hour and a half, which gave both Betty and George a long time, independently, to think through the situation. The police ploy of putting them in separate cars, of course, prevented them from collaborating to devise a consistent story. Both realised that although they were safe enough whilst in the custody of the police, there was an increasing possibility of the agents, who had promoted the attempted kidnap, learning of their location, which could put them in danger afterwards. Both also realised that since Betty had removed the photograph of herself from the kidnapper's pocket, there was actually nothing material to link the men in the crashed van with Betty and George, so that the police would presumably release them in due course after they had been interviewed. George, however, had an extra concern. He knew from his research in Modern History that there had been instances of unofficial connections and collaborations between the Austrian Security Police and Russian Intelligence. And particularly after the success of the far right in recent Austrian elections, its government now including members of the pro-Russian, far-right Freedom Party, those connections could exist without constraint. This amplified the chance of the would-be abductors becoming aware of their location, the longer they were in police custody.

George decided to engage in conversation with the officer driving him, hoping to steer the discussion round to politics to get a feel for that aspect of the situation. His driver turned out to be as fascinating with the anecdotes about Austrian culture as a first-class tour guide. After a while, they started talking about famous Austrians. George argued that Sigmund Freud could not be considered Austrian because he was born in what is now the Czech Republic, even though in the mid-1800s that was part of the Austrian empire. They both agreed that Christian Doppler and the great Erwin Schrödinger were authentically Austrian, though to the officer's surprise George used his historical knowledge to point out that Schrödinger's maternal grandmother was English; and the discovery of the Doppler effect was actually attributed to the French physicist, Frizeau, at least by the French themselves. From there, it was easy for George to steer the conversation to Austrian pride and its influence on politics. The officer was obviously enjoying the discussion but was ultimately unable to enlighten George on the political leanings of those in charge - apparently, it was not the sort of discussion subject that would be appropriate between officers and their superiors. As they reached the outskirts of the town of Villach, George's attention, as always, was drawn to the different architectures and the views of the wide river they were skirting, against the backdrop of mountains.

Betty had taken a different tack - she chatted amiably for a while to the female officer who had been charged with accompanying her, talking mainly about the skiing, reinforcing her image as a simple tourist who had met with some misunderstanding. But after a while, Betty took the opportunity to try to nap briefly in the car, having not had much sleep the previous night.

She started awake from a strange dream to see that it had now begun to snow quite heavily, and they were driving alongside a wide river, into a town in which there was a mix of modern buildings and older Alpine architecture. She asked the female officer, who explained it was the River Drava, they were now in Villach and would very soon be arriving at Stadtpolizeikommando.

Betty was accustomed to being very focussed and in control of her life. But since her fateful decision, and the unexpected dramatic events of this morning, she was embroiled in unfamiliar feelings - not totally understanding what was happening, or why. She felt somewhat irritated with the police officers being in control of events, and with gnawing anxiety about whether she might still be in danger from whatever agency had orchestrated the intended abduction.

They were led to separate interview rooms and given hot coffee. The Inspector interviewed first Betty, and then George. He started the interviews formally, declaring himself as Inspektor Matthias Schweiger, Bundespolizei Österreich. Now that the officers had removed their bulky winter coats, their uniforms were more apparent and imposing - Schweiger had impressive insignia emblazoned on the high collar of his jacket in true Germanic style. He asked essentially the same questions that he had earlier. Betty obliged by giving more graphic detail about her time at the crash scene, only omitting the details about the photo of herself, and the organic smell in the rear of the van. She made sure the Inspector understood that the stout man from the chalet next to the crash had endorsed her narrative about offering the gun to him first - so that she had in no way contrived to take the weapon. She also said that the man from the chalet would confirm that she was at the van within a minute of the crash, so could in no way have been involved in the accident itself, which was a mile back up the winding mountain road. George, for his part, simply repeated that he knew nothing about the crash other than what Betty had told him, as he had been asleep back in Heiligenblut. At length, this was all typed up into long statements, in English, that they were asked to read, and then sign.

George and Betty were then finally reunited, with a hug, in one of the interview rooms. "Thank you for your time," Schweiger said formally, handing back their passports that had been taken for recording details. "I am sorry for the disruption to your journey, but you understand we must investigate these things thoroughly. It has not been a good start to the year for those two poor men," he stated by way of justification.

"Mmm... who were they?" asked George, intrigued to see if there was an answer.

"We do not know yet," he replied. "Their bodies have been taken for autopsy to Klagenfurt. The van was registered in Romania - we are making enquiries. Officer Riegler will take you down to your car, though I must advise you that conditions on the road to Salzburg are not good at the moment, and the forecast is formidable. I would not advise to drive this afternoon." He gestured out of the window at the now heavily falling snow. "However there are many good hotels nearby if you decide to wait for better conditions tomorrow. Foreigners seem to like the Holiday Inn, which is close by." They were escorted down to collect their car from the police vehicle compound, and the female officer, Riegler, pointed out the directions to get to the main roads.

"Which way is the shopping area?" asked Betty.

"Well, there are plenty of small shops in the centre, just a kilometre that way, over the bridge, on the other side of the river. Or there is a big shopping mall called 'Atrio', about 3 kilometres down the main road in this direction," Officer Riegler gesticulated helpfully and good-naturedly.

"Thanks, that's really helpful," smiled Betty. George gently drove the car out of the police compound. "The Mall, James," joked Betty. "First task is to buy a new mobile phone, then we can sit down with some food, phone MI5, and use google-maps on the phone to find out where the hell we are." Betty was looking back. "I'm keeping an eye out, but I don't think we are being followed. I am wondering if we should return this car to the hire company and get a different one? - Then it would be even more difficult to trace us?"

George just grunted and nodded - he was focussing on the driving, as the snow was now making visibility very poor. But they soon found the Mall without difficulty, parked up and searched for a phone shop. Betty spent ages reading the specifications for each model, whilst George stood, bored and hungry. He had never understood the joys that some women find in shopping, which he wrongly assumed that Betty was indulging in, and felt that one smartphone was as good as any other. But he was generous enough not to hassle Betty, who was obviously engaged with the process. Finally, she found the one that satisfied her and bought it, also paying for some airtime, so that they could use it straight away. Then they walked around and found a noisy fast food outlet, where they could sit and converse, without fear of being overheard. Betty gratefully took a couple of bites of her burger, and then pulled out the new phone.

"Right, MI5 first." She keyed in the number.

"How do you know the number?" asked George incredulously.

"He called me back this morning - I memorised it as I couldn't take Hannah's phone with me. I'm a mathematician remember - numbers is what I do... Oh hi, is that Tom Wheatley? Yes, it's Betty Gosmore, from earlier."

"Betty, I'm glad to hear from you. I was worried. I called back to that phone you borrowed this morning, but someone named Hannah said you had returned it to her and left."

"Yes," confirmed Betty, "but this is a brand new phone I am on now, and it must presumably be secure, so if you store this number you can get me any time."

"Great, OK, Where are you now? At the airport?" continued Wheatley.

"Uh, I wish!" bemoaned Betty. "No, by chance we ran into the police as we drove by the crash scene, I got recognised, and then they found I had the gun, so they insisted on taking us back to their headquarters to make full statements. We are out now, but we are stuck in some town called..." She looked to George for the name.

"Villach," he supplied mechanically.

"Yes... Villach, and it's snowing quite hard, so I don't think we will be able to drive to Salzburg today."

"Right, I see. Did you tell the police it was a kidnap attempt?" asked Wheatley.

"No, that would just have got us in deeper," Betty hypothesised, "they seemed satisfied in the end that I was just a chance witness."

"OK, because," explained Wheatley, "it could complicate the safety issue somewhat if the police know where you are, since they will presumably be tracing the contacts, or next of kin, of the kidnappers."

"But the police would have no reason to tell the kidnappers about us would they?" Betty sounded alarmed.

"Agents are ruthless," clarified Wheatley, "they might tell the police that those guys have been hounded or whatever by a madwoman of your description... there are any number of scenarios they could use to delay your departure and get wind of your location..."

George, who had been following one side of the conversation, as he hungrily and gratefully consumed his burger, saw the sudden flash of worry cross Betty's face and beckoned for the phone.

"My colleague wants a word..." Betty informed Wheatley.

"Hi, I'm George Tremaine, Betty's friend. I have concerns about the police here because - I'm not sure whether you are aware - there are known to be links between the Austrian Security Police and Russian Intelligence." Betty was looking even more worried, hearing what George was saying.

"Yes, spot on George, we are aware of this," Wheatley reassured him, "so I am not going to call our counterparts in Austria unless it becomes absolutely necessary. The best solution is to get you out of the country as soon as possible, and in reality, it sounds like the risk to you is probably very small at the moment, but we should still do anything we can to minimise it."

"Betty suggested we return the hire-car and get a different one?" George queried.

"Yes, if you can get another car from a different hire company, anything to keep below the radar. Can I speak with Betty again?" George handed the phone back to Betty.

"Betty, do you still have that photo of yourself that was in one of the kidnappers' pockets?"

"Yes"

"Can you take a photo of it with your phone camera and message it to me please - that will help us in looking for clues as to how they pulled this stunt."

"OK."

"Now," Wheatley continued, "you said you are in Villach - well I see from my map that there is an airport in Klagenfurt which is much nearer than Salzburg. You might like to check out the flights from there. And can you phone me every couple of hours so I know exactly what's going on - you can get me on this phone 24/7."

"OK," replied Betty "We'll check out the airports and flights now, and get back to you when we have a plan then. Bye." She looked meaningfully at George "This is scary, George."

"Wheatley said the risk is probably very small, it's just that we need to do everything we can to minimise it." George was trying to sound reassuring.

"OK," she agreed, "Tom Wheatley said that there's another airport nearer, damn, I can't remember the name, something 'fart' I think." They both laughed. "I guess we need to get a map up on the phone next."

And a few minutes later they were delighted to discover that Klagenfurt airport was only 35 minutes drive away, and so they set about searching for possible flights back to the UK. "Look, it's a tiny airport, only five departures each day - it means extra connections, but that's worth it to save a long drive back up to Salzburg... Damn, there's only one more flight today, and no seats available... But look, there's a departure at 08:25 tomorrow morning to Cologne - that would get us out of the country, whereas the other 4 flights tomorrow all go up to Vienna. Then from Cologne, it would be easy to get back to the UK. Shall I book us onto that?"

"Well yes, but the other issue is the weather," considered George "We'd need to leave very early in the morning - check the forecast first." Betty deftly pulled the local weather forecast onto the phone screen.

"Well, the snow is expected to stop this evening, so they should have the roads clear by morning."

"OK, let's go for it," agreed George. "You book the flight, then I'll search for a hotel to hole up in for the night."

"But not the Holiday Inn," joked Betty. They both laughed. A plan had made all the difference to their morale. The next task was to switch the hire-car. George checked which hire firms were active both in Villach and at Klagenfurt airport, so that they would be able to return the new car. There was not much choice. The place where their current car needed to be returned, and the other hire firm, were in opposite directions, but only a few kilometres apart - Villach was not a large town.

"We'll have to pick up the new hire-car first," said George, "then we drive both cars to the place where we can return this one."

"Do you think it's worth it?" Betty sounded doubtful as she looked out of the window at the heavy snowfall.

"Yes, I do," replied George, "because one thing we haven't talked about is that there could be a tracker device somewhere on the car. If the would-be kidnappers were in Heiligenblut then they would have had plenty of opportunity to stick a magnetic one on the underside of our car."

"God, I hadn't thought of that." Betty was impressed. "Right let's

27

do it now - and get it over with."

The first sortie took them out of town to an industrial estate beside a massive railway marshalling yard. In the background there was a variety of unsettling metal on metal sounds, echoing across from the rail sidings, as trucks loudly protested being shoved around. The hiring administrator showing them the vehicles seemed, however, unfazed by the cacophony, presumably because he lived with it all day long. There were only 3 hire-vehicles to choose from. Because of the weather, Betty had no hesitation in choosing the large 4-wheel drive. She quickly familiarised herself with the controls and then gingerly followed George, who was driving their original car, through the deepening snow, back into town, past the police headquarters again and on for a couple of kilometres.

It happened suddenly in the last kilometre. Visibility was bad because of the snow falling. George had been regularly looking in the rear-view mirror to check that Betty was following, and then suddenly she wasn't there any more. With anxiety rising about another kidnap attempt, he slowed to a crawl - but she did not reappear in the rear-view mirror. He pulled the car abruptly over to the side of the road and jumped out, heart racing, running back without caution. He slipped. Because all around was white with snow, he momentarily lost his sense of orientation - it was as if the snow-covered pavement turned upward and struck him hard on the side of the head. Flashes of light accompanied the unhealthy thud that rattled his skull leaving an afterglow of ache. For a moment or two he felt an overwhelming sense of comfort and stillness just lying there, then transiently wondered if he had been shot, soon dismissing that thought for the overwhelmingly more plausible explanation that he had slipped and fallen. Then he remembered the urgent need to find Betty and gently manoeuvred himself into a squatting position so that he could try to stand again. He was thoroughly shaken and it took a couple of attempts before he got himself standing upright. His head and neck ached, and in truth, it might well have been much more serious, had his head impact not been partly cushioned by a couple of inches of fairly soft, fresh snow. Dazed and worried he steadied his legs and started back shakily, but much more carefully, along the side of the road to search for signs of Betty's car.

Meanwhile, Betty had been looking forward to the end of this leg of the journey, so that she could give all the driving back to George. Without warning, one of her involuntary jerks struck, her foot went down on the throttle, enough to spin the wheels up briefly, and the car slid sideways, ending up somewhere amongst the furrows of snow concealing the kerb. She cursed, and made a first unsuccessful attempt to straighten the car - one of the front wheels was up against the kerb, so that the other wheels just slid further round. With fear, she realised that she did not know the way to the car-hire office, or the hotel, without following George, and since he had the new phone, she had no way of contacting him. A car blared its horn as it passed, having to swerve around her. Seeing no other cars approaching she quickly backed up a foot or so and then accelerated at the kerb and bumped over it, allowing her to turn the car back to face the correct direction. Then she tentatively accelerated to try to catch up to George. She peered ahead anxiously as the wipers repeatedly swept the swirling snow off the windscreen, where it was being relentlessly replaced by still more. But quite soon, she spotted their original hire-car, parked up on the side of the road. With enormous relief, she pulled in gently behind it, flashed her lights and tooted the horn. Nothing. She did it again. Still no movement. She peered at the number plate, wondering if perhaps it might be a similar car, but not theirs? But yes, it was theirs. Not understanding, she reluctantly opened her car door and stepped out into the swirling snow to walk along and tap on George's car door window. No response and, as she peered in, anxiety rose up again inside her. She opened the door to double-check, but George was not there. Momentarily, panic shot through her as the thought intruded that maybe the kidnappers had struck, but quickly she weighed up the situation and realised that it was far more likely that George had just walked back down the road to try to find her. He could not have gone very far. She toyed with the idea of waiting for him to return, but decided that would be a bit unfair, so she reluctantly zipped up her ski jacket around her and started trudging back down the road. As she glanced down she noticed the fresh set of footprints which led from George's car - a direct connection to George. A smile crossed her face as she remembered her father teaching her basic tracking skills as a small child. She followed the footprints eagerly until they abruptly ended in a mishmash of disturbed snow. A frown crossed her brow - what had happened there? The footprints then seemed to resume on the other side of the disorder, so she resumed the pursuit, quickening her step, thankful that she was wearing snow boots that made the walking easy. Fairly soon she caught sight of a figure, indistinct through the falling snow, and soon was close enough to see it was indeed George walking rather awkwardly. "Hey," she shouted, "George..."

"Hey Betty, how did you get there? What happened? Are you

alright?"

"Yeah, I'm fine, I managed to spin the car sideways, but I caught you up after a minute or so and parked behind your car, you must have missed me as you were walking back?"

"God, yes," exclaimed George, "I was really worried the kidnappers might have struck again then... Ow!" he put his hand to his head - "I slipped over and banged my head."

"Oh my poor dear, yes, I saw from the tracks in the snow that something had happened. Are you OK?"

"Well I think so," conceded George, "I've got a stiff neck and a headache, but I'll survive."

She put her arm through his and led him tenderly back toward the cars. "I told you before we left, that you should have bought some proper boots - you can't expect to walk safely in snow with those brogues," she admonished him gently. "Are you going to be alright to drive?"

"Yes, it's only a short distance up this road now, on the right. God, what a day, I will be so relieved when we get to the hotel and can relax."

"Indeed, but remember I got much less sleep than you last night," Betty reminded him. "Right, here we are." As they arrived back at the two cars, she vigorously brushed off the snow from George's jacket and head. "Let's get rid of as much snow as we can so it doesn't steam up the insides of the windows." They settled into the two cars and slowly re-started the convoy to the car-hire office.

A few minutes later they had returned the small hire-car, completed the ubiquitous paperwork and got on their way in the 4-wheel drive. "So where is this hotel you booked for us, George?" queried Betty. "Oh, we're not going back past the police headquarters again? - Can't we go a different route?" pleaded Betty, as George turned back the way they had come.

"Best to keep to the main roads in this snow," countered George. "Don't worry, it's the last time, because the hotel I booked is nicely situated to drive straight on to the South Autobahn tomorrow morning, taking us directly to the airport... And the hotel has a surprise."

"Oh?" Betty sounded intrigued but didn't push for an explanation.

About a quarter of an hour later, they pulled into the car park of the Hotel Warmbaderhof. It was a sprawling but stylish collection of traditional and modern architecture in very large grounds. "OK, so what's the surprise?" asked Betty looking round as they walked into the grand foyer.

"Well, it's a spa, built over a natural hot spring, so lots of swimming pools."

"Oh," Betty sounded pleased. "But I didn't pack a bikini for a skiing holiday, George!"

"No problem." George nodded over to one side where a hotel shop sported swimming costumes amongst other expensive looking garments. "...And," he continued, "the hotel has a piano in one of the lounges."

"Oh, brilliant," Betty's face had lit up. "...And," she parroted, looking at the information on the reception counter, "they do massages, so you can get your neck-ache fixed." Suddenly the day was seeming a lot more promising.

At Betty's request, the receptionist was able to schedule an immediate massage for George. Meanwhile, after dropping their bags in their room, Betty sought out the piano lounge and gently eased herself into an impromptu recitation of Lizst's 'Années de pèlerinage', much to the appreciation of a few hotel residents who were relaxing on the spacious, comfortable sofas around the lounge. The black Grand piano, crowned with a candelabrum and vase of flowers, was standing on a sumptuous burgundy rug, atop polished marble tiles, and was fronted by an artistic contemporary cluster of low-hanging globe lights which were reflecting in the tiles. The effect was both luxurious and aesthetic, and the perfect tuning of the piano buoyed and satisfied Betty, being incomparably better than the small-town church piano that she had been playing in Heiligenblut for the last few days. She soon became completely absorbed in the music, and reinvigorated, oblivious to the surroundings. Following his massage, George searched out the lounge and relaxed back in one of the sumptuous armchairs near to the piano, listening.

The snow had finally all but stopped, and the next hour found them alone, resting at the edge of a hot outdoor swimming pool, gazing at the beautiful scenery, and enjoying the unexpected juxtaposition of outdoors and hot water. The snow-covered lawn stretched away from the far side of the pool to a vista of diversely shaped trees, each branch outlined with a covering of snow, like a traditional Christmas card picture, whilst the occasional snowflake tumbled its way into the pool to melt instantly in the hot mineral-rich water. Breaks in the cloud now allowed irregular patches of blue sky to mirror the blue of the pool itself. They were silent for a long time, savouring the unexpected beauty at the end of a harrowing day.

"Well I guess we are well off the radar now," mused Betty at length. "Thank you for finding such a lovely hotel, George. How's your head?

"Mostly better, thanks. Yes, it almost seems just like an extension of the holiday here, after a bad dream."

"Damn," said Betty remembering, "I forgot to check in with Tom Wheatley - he wanted me to phone every couple of hours. Well, I'm not getting out of this beautiful pool just to make a phone call - he'll have to wait until I'm good and ready."

George laughed. "It will be getting dark soon."

"I'm sure they have some lights to switch on," she argued. "I might just lie in here all night - except that I am already getting a bit hungry," she added ruefully. "Do you think the police were being malevolent today, George, dragging us all the way to the police station?"

"No," he considered, "it's part of the German-Austrian psyche that they are punctilious - they need to get an interview and everything written into a report." He laughed. "I have seen it reported that 40% of the Austrians applying for early retirement on health grounds are bureaucrats - they take it all, *that* seriously. Of course, your gun didn't help!"

Betty laughed.

Just as dusk began to steal away the charm from the scene, the lights did indeed come on giving a fresh take on the panorama, now striking and designed. But after a few minutes, it was clear that the synthetic vista could not compete with the earlier natural perfection, and so they decided to return to their room before dinner.

"Hello Tom, it's Betty Gosmore again... yes, sorry, we were relaxing in the pool. So, we have switched the hire-car for another...

Yes, a different company… We were definitely not followed - the snow was so heavy we could barely follow each other. So now we are holed up in a beautiful hotel, ready to leave first thing in the morning for Klagenfurt airport - we have booked flights from there to Cologne, and we can easily get a flight from Cologne to the UK. I'm feeling much safer now."

"OK, that all sounds good Betty. So that photo you took from the kidnapper and copied to me - you said you didn't recognise it - but can you tell where it was taken?"

"Oh OK, let me have another look." She reached into her pocket, pulled out the photo and studied it. "No, I'm sorry, I don't recognise where it is - there's not much background to go on. But the photo can't be too old - I'm wearing a coat that I bought at the end of last summer."

"We have zoomed in on it here and it looks like there is a display of electronic goods behind you. Is that any help?"

"Um… no, but I'll have a think about it."

"OK, well I'll assume you are safe overnight - though you can get me on this number 24 hours if you need to - will you call me again when you get on the road tomorrow morning please?"

"Yes sure Tom, OK goodbye…" She put the phone away. "Right, he's happy. Now, a nice meal and an early night?"

The evening proved to be so pleasant after the stressful day, and so much like a continuation of their holiday that George was not motivated to ask Betty for the promised explanation of why she had been driving away from Heiligenblut, and indeed away from him, early in the morning. At that moment it seemed rather irrelevant - after all, she was with him now. Similarly, Betty was disinclined to break the atmosphere in order to broach a difficult subject, and so the matter remained unexplained and unresolved between them.

Chapter 3
The Hospital Room and a new Weapon

MONDAY 2nd January

Dawn the next morning saw the weather much improved, and after a breakfast, George and Betty slung their bags into the four-wheel-drive at first light, and set off. Visibility was now fine, and although George drove tentatively on the local road because it was still snow-covered, when they got to the autobahn they were relieved to find it had been cleared overnight. Once up to speed on the autobahn, Betty phoned Tom Wheatley to confirm that they were on their way. The airport was easy to find and only a half-hour journey. They returned the hired four-wheel-drive, then trundled their bags into the hall of the tiny airport to find the check-in desk. They had got used to the meticulous bureaucratic and deliberate manner in which administration was conducted in Austria, but there was something about the way that the woman behind the desk was dealing with their passports that unsettled George. Betty noticed two Austrian police officers striding purposefully toward the check-in desk. She quickly pulled the phone out of her pocket and called Tom Wheatley. "Hi Tom, we are at the airport check-in now, I think we may have some more trouble, can you hang on..." She kept the phone to her ear.

The first police officer looked at the passports that the check-in clerk handed him, and turned to George and Betty. "Mees Gosmore and Herr Tremaine, we are to take you to Stadtpolizeikommando. The Inspektor wishes to interview you."

Betty's heart dropped, yet also some anger rose in her. "But he interviewed us yesterday - there is nothing more to tell him."

The officer shook his head. "I think there are new developments, madam, you must come with us."

"What new developments?" Betty demanded.

"Put the phone away please madam."

"Did you catch all that Tom?" Betty said into her phone.

"Yes," replied Wheatley. "Call me from the police station when you can." She felt a little safer that at least Wheatley knew where they would be.

George meanwhile, had been checking what was visible of the police uniforms - they certainly seemed consistent with the uniforms he had seen yesterday. His first worry that they might be agents, rather than police, seemed unfounded. But all the worry and frustration of yesterday came crashing back, and with it that headache of his that had never quite gone away.

The woman behind the check-in desk looked at them blankly, then she turned to the next people in line as Betty and George were marched off to a police car parked outside. Their bags were stowed in the boot and they were searched for weapons before being put in the back seat. They said nothing to each other on the drive back to Villach. Betty was angry. George was despondent, and had the uneasy feeling that he should not have been making disparaging statements about Austrian bureaucracy the previous night.

When they arrived at the police station, Betty's anger was fuelled further on hearing that Inspector Schweiger would not be arriving for work for another half an hour. They were put in a room together to wait and given coffee.

"What on earth do you think they want with us now?" demanded Betty, wincing at the taste of the coffee.

"I've no idea," George replied, shaking his head palpably - a signal intended to convey to Betty that it would definitely be a bad idea to speculate on the issue within earshot of the police officer in the room. Betty occupied herself with texting the lack of progress to Tom Wheatley, and catching up with the news on her phone. Finally, she was lead to an interview room where Schweiger was now waiting.

"So why have you brought us back here again? That is the second flight home you have caused me to miss." Betty wasted no time in showing her irritation.

Schweiger smiled inwardly - it was always easier to get the truth from someone when they were angry. But he himself felt insulted. "Because you lied to me yesterday. You think you can lie to the police

36

and then sneak out of Austria?"

"I did *not* lie," countered Betty flatly.

"I asked you if you knew either of the men who were killed in the van," insisted Schweiger. "You answered 'no'. But yesterday afternoon we received here the belongings of the dead men, and in those belongings, we found no less than five photographs of yourself. So clearly you *did* know them."

Betty allowed some surprise to show on her face. She had not considered that there might be additional photographs, other than the one that she had removed from the van, even though in retrospect it was not that surprising. And, in the same instant, she was realising that it was best to act as if this were a revelation, since she had concealed the existence of the first photograph from Schweiger.

"No, Inspector Schweiger, your logic is faulty," retorted Betty sharply. "What those photos prove is that those men knew *me*, the photos do not demonstrate that I knew *them*. Indeed, I did *not* know them; I had never seen them before. I did not lie to you."

The Inspector seemed momentarily surprised at the flat denial. "Do not toy with me madam, why would these men have photos of you, indeed be following you on the road, if there is no connection between you and them?"

"Indeed Inspector, what would you suspect is the motive of men with a gun, and photos of a person, following that person on a quiet road?" Betty responded rhetorically.

"I might suspect," replied Schweiger, playing along, "that their intentions are not good, but as for the motive - that is what I am asking you. Whether you knew them or not is a secondary issue."

"It is not a secondary issue - you accused me of lying." Betty was determined not to let that pass.

"Ah, OK, OK, perhaps I was too hasty in making that assumption," conceded Schweiger. "But you must understand that I can only work with the facts that are available to me, which clearly indicate a connection between you and these men. I cannot allow you to leave until I am clear that there has been no foul play on your part, but at the moment I cannot establish the facts in this case. You seem to be suggesting to me that you are an intended victim in all this. If you can help me by explaining the motive of these men - and I strongly believe that you do have knowledge of that motive - then perhaps I can get closer to resolving the case, and you can get closer to returning home?"

Betty leaned back and sighed, considering the situation. She was no longer angry - it was clear that Schweiger had not been unreasonable, given the facts at his disposal, and she had made her point about not lying. It seemed unavoidable now that he would have to be told the whole story, or at least most of it.

"OK Inspector Schweiger, I need to give you information in confidence - could you turn off the recording machine please." The Inspector looked surprised - but complied by clicking off the machine - he would be only too pleased to get the information he needed to clarify this case, whichever way she chose to give it to him. Betty turned to the female officer who was also sitting in the room - "I'm sorry - would you mind?" she apologised. Schweiger nodded to the officer, and she stood and left the room, looking unmistakably disappointed.

Schweiger leaned back in his chair, cocking his head questioningly.

"I work for the UK government intelligence service. I have knowledge of very sensitive secret information. I was on holiday here. I knew nothing of these men until the crash. I can only assume that the men were intending to kidnap and abduct me to extract information from me. And so I also have to assume that my own anonymity has been breached, and I am therefore vulnerable until I can get back to the UK."

Schweiger raised his eyebrows and took a deep breath.

"What sort of secret information?" he queried, attempting to probe further.

"Obviously I can not be any more explicit." Betty dismissed the question curtly.

Schweiger smiled.

Betty moved to close the conversation. "Clearly you will want confirmation of my status from the UK security authorities - I'm not sure of the protocol - I can phone them now - is there any particular official you would like them to contact?"

Schweiger nodded. "OK. Yes, phone your UK security police now - I do not know what the communication lines are - but I assume we would, in due course, get a phone call from my superior."

Betty pulled out her phone and called MI5. "Hello Tom, it's Betty again, yes... Look, I have had to explain to Inspector Schweiger here, that I am assuming this was a kidnap attempt. Yes... Well his officers found several photos of me on the dead men, which establishes a link between them and me, so he can't let me leave until he establishes the full facts - can you contact the Austrian police command to let Inspector Schweiger know that what I have said about my identity and situation is true?... OK." She passed the phone over to the Inspector at Wheatley's request.

"Hello, yes... Yes, Inspektor Schweiger," he spelled out the name, "Ja... Stadtpolizeikommando, Villach. Ja... Ja... OK Danke, Auf Wiedersehen Herr Wheatley." He handed the phone back to Betty.

"Your Mr Wheatley is very polite, and he speaks good German," grinned Schweiger. "He has suggested me that I must give you police protection until you leave our country. So, now tell me about your friend, Herr Tremaine - he is your bodyguard?"

"Goodness, no," laughed Betty, "he is a work colleague, and in the same position as myself with regard to sensitive information and vulnerability. He is also a very close friend."

"Ha, I see, well I will go and talk with him now, whilst we wait for the phone call to confirm your identity and situation. Officer Riegler will come in and sit with you again." He left the room sending Riegler back in.

"I'm sorry I had to ask you to leave the room," proffered Betty, as the female officer returned. Kathi Riegler just shrugged. Betty felt some concern - although it was wise to restrict her information to the smallest number of people possible, it was however not a good idea to raise curiosity, rumour or resentment in these other officers. She started some small-talk in an attempt to heal the wound.

Meanwhile, Schweiger returned to the room where George was waiting. He found George with his head in his hands. The police officer, who had been stationed in the room with George, explained that George was not feeling well, and had been sick in the toilet.

Schweiger seemed genuinely concerned. "Oh dear," he addressed the officer, "let's get Miss Gosmore back in here."

Betty was immediately alarmed when she was brought back in. "Let me see your eyes, George," she said sitting down in front of him.

"It's this damn headache," mumbled George, "and it's making me feel sick."

Betty turned to Schweiger. "He slipped over yesterday and

banged his head. The pupils of his eyes are normal, thank god, but - I think he might have a concussion. I wonder if we ought to get him checked over in a hospital?"

Schweiger nodded. "Yes, yes, it's best to be vigilant with head injuries. Officer Riegler will drive you both to Landeskrankenhaus - the hospital - it is only one kilometre up the road. But please do not try to leave - consider that you remain under detention for the moment, until I am satisfied by the message from my superiors that we are waiting for. Officer Riegler will stay at the hospital with you - I will let you know when I hear."

George seemed sullen and fragile as Betty led him down the stairs and out to the police car. It was only a few minutes to the hospital. Betty, having translated Landeskrankenhaus as best she could, was anticipating a small country hospital; and so she was rather relieved and heartened to discover that it was actually a large modern complex. But her relief quickly turned to concern when George, looking up at the building as they drove through the entrance, mumbled, "Which airport is this?"

It might have been Austrian efficiency, or the time of day, but it seemed to Betty that being accompanied by a uniformed police officer facilitated getting them seen by a doctor very quickly. The ER consultant took in their story of a fall, headache, sickness and confusion and made some notes. When she heard that George had taken aspirin for the headache last night and that morning, she shook her head reprovingly, and explained that aspirin can exacerbate bleeding and bruising in the brain, and was not a good idea. She decided that he should have a CT scan as a precaution, and prescribed him some more appropriate pain relief. There was an hour wait for the scan - George sat dourly in silence, whilst Betty chatted to Kathi Riegler. Towards the end of the hour, Kathi Riegler took a call from Schweiger. "Ja... Ja Inspektor... Ja... OK." she handed the phone to Betty.

"Ah, Miss Gosmore," he started, "as we expected I have received a call from my superiors in Vienna, who are confirming that you and Herr Tremaine are a kidnap risk for the reason you stated, and that I should facilitate your return to the UK as soon as possible, and close the case here. So how is Herr Tremaine - is he fit to travel?"

"We are not sure yet - the doctor has arranged for a CT scan, which should happen soon - actually he is being called in now," she added as a medic entered the area that they were waiting in, and called his name, struggling with the pronunciation. Kathi Riegler laughed, and led George over to the door, jokingly castigating the medic's efforts at English articulation.

"Oh dear," Schweiger continued on the phone. "OK, well let me know as soon as you get news. I would like to get you away from here as soon as possible otherwise the Bundeskriminalamt - that is the federal police here - will want to take over, and, well I'm not sure you are interested in our politics here in Austria, but there are some tensions between some of the politically-controlled police sections and... But I have said too much already. The sooner we get you out of the country, the sooner we can all relax. Now, I will have to give instructions to Officer Riegler that she is now protecting you rather than detaining you, and that the possible, though unlikely, threat is from armed foreign agents, so that she is prepared. But of course, I will only brief her, or any other officer who *needs* to know. Can I speak with her again now please?"

Betty handed the phone back to Kathi Riegler, who listened to her Inspector for a couple of minutes, occasionally interjecting "Ja..." Betty watched her facial expression and thought she probably identified the point when Schweiger explained about the kidnap risk, as Kathi's eyebrows rose, and subconsciously her hand reached down to check her holstered gun. Betty smiled - it was comforting to feel protected.

Putting her phone away, Kathi turned to Betty with a smile. "Ah, so you are making our job more interesting, I had no idea."

"I'm sorry I couldn't tell you before," apologised Betty.

"No, I completely understand," Kathi assured her. "Schweiger is a bit concerned about the responsibility - he realises it would have been easier all round if we had let you get on the aeroplane this morning, but he only had half the picture then."

George was brought back in about 15 minutes, still feeling a bit nauseous, though he said the painkillers were beginning to kick in, and relieving his headache a bit. The consultant returned a few minutes later and called them into a side office. "Well, you are not good at keeping still, are you, Mr Tremaine?" she castigated him mildly, looking at the slightly fuzzy scan image on a computer screen. "There is nothing major wrong at the moment, although I can see a little bruising on the side of the brain. I would suggest we keep you here under observation for 24 hours to make sure nothing serious develops from it."

Betty and Kathi looked at each other. "So he is not fit to travel today?" asked Kathi.

"I would advise against it," the consultant shook her head. "If any serious bleed develops he needs to have medical help available promptly, and it's best if he keeps his head still today. If nothing comes of it in the next 24 hours then he will likely be fine to travel, though it can sometimes take a week or more to feel completely back to normal after a concussion."

"Well," mused Betty, "having missed the early morning flight from Klagenfurt, today's only other option would be the two-hour drive to Salzburg, or maybe Graz airport, which doesn't sound like a good idea."

Kathi nodded. "So," she asked the consultant, "would it be OK to discharge him early tomorrow morning, so he can catch the early flight?"

"If he has shown no adverse symptoms by then, yes, that should be fine," she concurred, and she stood to leave.

"It's very important he has a private room," Kathi stated firmly.

"Oh!... OK, yes, I can arrange that," agreed the consultant, slightly surprised, but deferring to the credibility that Kathi's uniform bestowed.

George, meanwhile, was taking this all in, but feeling rather detached, strangely content, on the painkillers, whilst the three women organised his life for him.

Once they were all installed into a private room, Kathi Riegler phoned Inspector Schweiger to update him on the situation and arrangements. He was not pleased at the 24-hour delay, extending his responsibility and anxiety. Betty, likewise, phoned Tom Wheatley to let him know the new situation. Tom's voice always conveyed warmth and reliability though he too, seemed concerned at the prolonged exposure to potential danger. "Listen, Betty, I am going to send an agent down from Vienna. He may not contact you directly but he will be around to keep an eye on things just in case there is any problem. If he does need to make contact with you, he will use the code phrase - '*The snow seems to deaden the shadows here.*' And when we end this call I will send you a text with a link in it - just click on the link, that will activate tracking, and then he and I will be able to track your new phone to know where you are at all times."

"It's that easy is it?" asked Betty.

"Well to be honest we could do it without that, so long as we know the number - it just makes it simpler, so that we don't have to hack the network suppliers!" Wheatley laughed.

That phone call reminded Betty of something, gave her a new idea, and she spent some time thinking deeply, staring vacantly out of the hospital room window. The nurse, who had shown them into the room, returned again and attended to measuring George's pulse, blood pressure and temperature and recording them on his chart. She asked him which of the items on the menu he would like for lunch and if he wanted a drink, which he declined, but she did not ask Betty and Kathi - this further fuelled Betty's nascent idea. She spent a couple of minutes using Google Maps on her phone, before turning to Kathi.

"So Kathi," began Betty, "George will clearly be getting his meals from the nursing staff, but we'll have to go and find our own, won't we?"

"Um, I guess so," replied Kathi. "There's a canteen downstairs in the hospital. I can go and fetch some food for you if you don't want to be seen?"

"I was actually thinking the opposite," replied Betty, "that if it's safe enough for us to go to the canteen, then it would be safe enough to go to a café just down the road. You see, the Cafeteria Nikolai is an internet café and I desperately want to do a little bit of work on a computer - it's literally only a hundred metres from the corner of this block?"

"Oh, I'm not sure we should do that," objected Kathi.

"So what is your protocol for protecting us then?" asked Betty. "I mean if you go down to the canteen you are leaving us on our own here, and it sounded as if you thought it would be all right for me to accompany you to the canteen?"

"Um, I'm not certain, to be honest," replied Kathi. "We've never had to do this before. Inspector Schweiger just told me to stay with you, and I don't really want to pester him on details. We just need to be sensible."

"OK then, let's have a sensible early lunch at Café Nikolai, before it gets crowded, nobody would know to come looking for me there anyway, you will be with me, and George will be safe enough tucked away in here."

Kathi thought about it for a few moments. "OK, let's go now, but only for a very short while." Betty had been expecting to have to argue further or even walk out to get her way, but Kathi seemed surprisingly relaxed about her role.

The two women strode briskly out of the hospital entrance, following a path skirting around the back of the car park which was outlined on the map on Betty's phone, efficiently finding NikolaiStrasse and the cafe within a couple of minutes. A small shabby man furtively left as soon as he saw Kathi walk in and noticed her uniform. Betty made a beeline for one of the tables with a computer, and Kathi called over the waiter, apologising and laughing over the hasty exit of his surreptitious customer. She ordered a couple of Wiener schnitzel and looked around attentively, sipping her coffee whilst Betty tinkered furiously on the keyboard.

"What are you doing?" queried Kathi in a way that expressed both admiration and amusement at Betty's industriousness.

"Mmm... I'm building an interface between my phone and work," she mumbled without looking up.

The Schnitzels arrived. Betty absently forked a first piece into her mouth, still attentive to the computer screen. But on tasting it, she looked up and smiled at Kathi, "Hey, this is good." She had plugged her phone into the computer, and was now tapping characters on the screen and watching the responses that appeared on the computer screen. At length, she seemed satisfied, and concentrated on the eating.

A call came through on Kathi's phone - Inspector Schweiger was asking her some questions. "Ah," she replied, "that evidence is still with forensics... Yes, those documents are still on my desk." Then, still listening, she stiffened visibly. She rose. "Quick, we need to get back to the hospital - Schweiger is coming over," she explained, pulling some money out of her pocket, and dropping it on the table for the waiter.

"Let me pay for mine," protested Betty.

"Later, we need to hurry," and she tugged on Betty's arm as Betty conscientiously logged off and switched off the screen. The two women walked briskly back into the hospital grounds.

"What has happened?" asked Betty with concern.

"There has been a development - Schweiger needs to ask you some more questions. Best you don't tell him we left the hospital," was all that Kathi would say.

They got back to George's room, finding him napping

comfortably on the bed. Kathi was visibly relieved to find they had got back before Schweiger had arrived, and she relaxed a bit. In fact, it was a full 10 minutes later before Schweiger arrived, by which time the two women had fully recovered their composure after half-jogging back from their clandestine adventure.

Kathi stood when Schweiger entered the room and gave him her chair.

"Right," he began, less formally than he talked in his interview room, "there has been a strange development - I am a bit confused, and I am hoping you can enlighten me. You see there has been, what appears to be, another kidnap attempt, but on the outskirts of Villach this time. Now if I say this is rare - well, in fact, I can't remember the last time we dealt with a kidnap. So I am assuming this must be connected to your incident yesterday. So my question is: Were there any other of your colleagues holidaying with you, or in this area?" He had angled his chair so that he could see both Betty's and George's faces, and he looked from one to the other questioningly.

George, still befuddled with pain-killers, said simply, "No, it was only us."

Betty's brow furrowed slightly as she struggled to understand the complication. "We're not aware that anyone else was holidaying here, though it is possible as a coincidence. Do you know *who* was abducted?" she asked.

"Not yet, I've got four officers down there at the scene right now, gathering information. Anyway, the other issue I need to sort out is the arrangement for tonight. Herr Tremaine will obviously be here in this room - did you want to stay in this room also, Miss Gosmore, or are you hoping for a hotel room?"

"No, I think it's better if we stay together here - I can sleep in the chair," offered Betty.

"Oh, I am sure the hospital will find another bed to put in this room if Officer Riegler asks them?" He turned to face Kathi, who nodded assent.

"Now, Officer Riegler," he continued, "I will send another officer over here to relieve you at 20:00 this evening. So, get some sleep then, if you can, and please come back on duty here at 06:00 and you can drive our guests to the airport first thing in the morning. Is that OK?"

"Yes, sir."

Inspector Schweiger's phone rang, and he took the call, pacing randomly in the relatively small hospital room, as he listened to the information from his officers at the scene. "Ja... Lokal frau?... Ja..."

He held the phone away from his face for a moment while he gave a commentary to the others in the room. "It seems they drove a local woman off the road, bundled her into their van, but then put her out of the van again only a kilometre up the road. Crazy. Maybe it is not connected after all."

"Ask them the registration plate of the woman's vehicle, sir," put in Kathi who seemed to be thinking a step ahead.

Schweiger clearly valued Riegler's input. He asked the question over the phone and recited the answer back to Kathi Riegler, who turned to Betty for confirmation. Betty had her hand to her mouth, "Oh God, yes, that was our original hire-car... Poor woman, she must have been terrified." Although Betty's sympathy was genuine, it sprung from resonance with a surge of fear she was herself feeling right now.

"Ha, so," Schweiger nodded, "excellent anticipation, Riegler. We will almost certainly find a tracking device on that car - good hard evidence of intent, but it will probably not help us to find the attackers - though we will, of course, follow the leads that we have. It is some small comfort that they thought you were still driving that car - it means they do not know where you are. Hopefully, they will now conclude that you have left Austria and will refrain from any further activity here."

Schweiger left, apparently satisfied that this mystery had been clarified. Betty, however, was rattled. On the one hand, she was heartened by the idea that, as Schweiger had articulated, they obviously did not know where she was, but on the other hand it was unnerving to acknowledge their persistence.

Kathi relaxed again and sat back down in one of the chairs, unzipping her navy blue uniform jacket. "Wow, they do keep the inside of hospitals very warm," she commented. "But I suppose we shouldn't complain - we have good health."

Betty smiled in agreement. "And, in Schweiger, you have a boss that treats you respectfully - he actually values your input. Back in England, my boss doesn't think women are capable of contributing ideas."

"Does he just tell you what to do then?" asked Kathi.

Betty snorted. "No, he has no real understanding of what we do -

we just get on with it ourselves. We are scientists, he is just an... administrator." Betty stumbled on the last word, remembering that George had said how the Austrians really valued bureaucracy, but Kathi just laughed.

"Is that the way it is in England generally then, with ignorant people in charge?" asked Kathi.

"Oh, no, that's just our project," responded Betty. "But I'm not complaining - I absolutely love my job - it's incredibly interesting."

"I suppose you are not allowed to tell me what you do?" queried Kathi.

"No, that's right," Betty smiled, "I *can* tell you I am a mathematician, but that's all." Kathi nodded. "How about you Kathi, do you enjoy your job?" Betty reciprocated.

"Yes, I love it," Kathi replied. "Every day is different, and Schweiger is very open about the details of cases, so it's easy to learn."

"And the uniform is cool," added Betty. "I must admit I have a thing about uniforms. Especially the beret. I think the outdoor image with sunglasses and beret works perfectly." Kathi laughed and threw her beret across to Betty so that she could try it on.

"No, no," said Kathi watching. "It doesn't look right like *that* - we have to tie our hair back first."

Betty retrieved a hair band from her pocket, tied her hair back and went to try on the beret using the bathroom mirror. When she had it just right, she took a selfie. It occurred to her, in passing, that a police uniform might make a very good disguise if the kidnappers did get close. She returned the beret to Kathi and stepped over to the bed to check on George. He was peacefully asleep again - the nurse had advised her that he would probably sleep most of the day because of the sedative effect of the medication.

As she sat down in her chair again, she was surprised to see, through the window, a red and white helicopter flying in close to the hospital, though the sound was not too invasive because of the double-glazing on the windows.

"Ah, there's a helicopter landing pad on the roof," explained Kathi. "It's probably an accident rescue from the mountains. We have a lot of ski runs a few miles north of here - on Gerlitzen. I go up there myself sometimes. There's a beautiful hotel right at the top with an outdoor pool, and an observatory for when the nights are cloudless. It's one of my most favourite places - the air is just so clean up there. And the views, looking down on Villach in the distance, or down on the huge Ossiacher Lake, are just stunning."

"Oh, you have a lake here as well?" echoed Betty.

"Well several nearby actually," expanded Kathi, "so all kinds of water sports, and we don't only use the mountains for skiing - in the summer there is paragliding, hiking, biking and so on. It's a wonderful place to live, or to holiday. Perhaps you could come back here for a holiday another time, when all this nonsense is sorted out?"

"Oh... well..." Betty suddenly looked downcast. "I'm not sure, now that my anonymity has been breached, I may never be able to go abroad again. But even if I could..." She tailed off.

Kathi saw the tears in Betty's eyes. "Oh, I'm so sorry, that was insensitive of me," she apologised.

"No, no, it's not your fault. It's not just the security issue, there is another reason." Betty glanced over at George. She felt that she wanted to confide in Kathi, though not in front of George, as she still had not explained it to him yet. But he seemed to be fast asleep. She lowered her voice. "You see I have a progressive health problem. I may not have much more time." She doubled over, bursting into tears. Kathi came over and put her arm around Betty as, between sobs, Betty explained her illness and her decision.

"So I've known for a long time that this was coming, and I've always been clear with myself that I would live my life abundantly until the time came, and then I would just end it, because I don't want a drawn-out miserable decline like I saw my father go through. And up until a month or so ago, I was fine, really enjoying everything. Then the signs came. But I kept faith with myself; I planned my trip to the assisted suicide clinic in Zurich, for yesterday. I was clear about what I wanted. And then all this happened - the hardest decision I have had to make in my life, and it's as if these barbarians, whoever they are, just totally disrespect me and trash my resolve. Now I'm simply confused and wanting to go home. I'm not even sure now that it would be safe for me to travel abroad to Zurich, assuming I manage to regain my calm and resolve. I feel as if my whole spirit has been compromised."

Kathi was a sympathetic listener, and Betty opened up to her, also relating many of the good and valued experiences she had lived. Kathi, in turn, talked about some of the more difficult times in her life, and their conversation and relationship deepened until some time later, a male officer arrived, midway through the afternoon, to cover Kathi for her break. He insisted on sitting on a chair outside the hospital room while he attended, so Betty decided to take the opportunity to make an important private call to Alex. However, mindful that *his* phone might also have been hacked, she called him via his wife, Petra's, number.

"Hi Petra, it's Betty here... Happy New Year... yes, we've had a great time - there's lots of good snow. Look, sorry, is Alex there? I need to speak to him - it's quite important. Thanks." There was a pause. Betty could hear Petra taking one of the children from Alex and sending him to the phone.

"Hi Alex... yes... Listen, yes, we've had a good time here but there has also been a bit of trouble. There was an attempt to kidnap me." There was a sharp intake of breath on the other end. "No, It's OK, I'm fine, luckily they had an accident before they got to me, and I'm under Austrian police protection now. But we can't leave here right at the moment because George had a fall yesterday and is in hospital with a concussion. I'll fill you in on all the details when we get back. But it looks like my phone was hacked - that's why I'm calling you on a new phone via Petra - in case yours is hacked too - so be careful what you say over your own phone until it's sorted out... Yes, MI5 are on to it.

"But listen, Alex, this is what I called to talk to you about. When I coded up the software for the i-vector equipment back at the lab, I programmed a back door into it, in case I ever wanted to run it remotely from my phone. Could you do me a favour and make sure the equipment is switched on please, in the instability range, just in case I need to use it. Do you understand what I am asking?"

Betty had deliberately avoided being explicit over the phone in case the call was monitored. There was a moment's silence as the meaning of Betty's request became clear to Alex - she was intending to use her phone to be able to remotely instantiate zaps from the i-vector equipment, thus using her phone as a deadly weapon. "Jesus, are you sure, Betty? That's really dangerous," he protested.

"Yes, I do realise that," Betty assured him. "I won't use it unless I absolutely need to. And I probably won't need to because I've got a police officer looking after me. But this is very serious Alex, there are people after me with guns."

"But how would you set the correct coordinates?" demanded Alex.

"I'll just use my smartphone's own GPS coordinates with an

49

appropriate offset - say two metres in front of me," explained Betty

"But smartphone coordinates are not nearly accurate enough," argued Alex. "They can be off by anything up to 10 metres."

"Aha," countered Betty, rather relishing the opportunity to win this tiny academic debate with Alex, "but I bought this particular model of phone today especially because it's got the new Broadcom dual-frequency high-accuracy GPS chip in it - accurate to within a few centimetres."

"Uh, fair enough, OK then." Alex acquiesced with a sigh. "I think Harriet is off, she's taken a week's holiday over the New Year so for the next couple of days at least, it should be available all the time for you. I'll go into the lab now and start the equipment running. But be careful. And tell George to get well soon. Is there anything else I can do to help?"

"Thank you Alex. No, that's all - just be careful what you say on your own phone - I expect the security people will contact you soon to check it. Hopefully, I'll see you later tomorrow or the next day, once we can get a flight out of here. Thank you honey, bye." Her voice cracked on the last words as tears entered her eyes. Just yesterday, she remembered, she was expecting never to see Alex again, but right now she was so valuing his comradeship and help. This sudden, forced transition from yesterday's hard decision, to today's vulnerability and dependence, was raking her emotions.

Betty then made use of the time while Kathi was still absent, to study the map of Villach on her phone, and memorise the locations of useful places nearby - 'just in case', she told herself - a bike-hire shop, a car-hire lot, the train station and departure times. She didn't imagine she would have occasion to use the information - she and George should be departing via the airport early in the morning. Finally, she downloaded an ebook and started to read it on her phone.

Kathi reappeared shortly before 5 o'clock, to Betty's relief - she had been getting very bored sitting around alone. At least Kathi talked to her - the male officer who had been guarding them during the afternoon break had simply sat on a chair, outside the room, the whole time, and George, drowsy from the medication, had just been mostly dozing in the bed.

Kathi explained that she had been incorporating the fingerprint data, which had this afternoon come back from the lab, into another case report that she was working on, before grabbing a bit of shopping. They were soon engrossed in conversation again.

Chapter 4
The Walkabout

Later that evening Inspector Schweiger had returned home after the day's work and was getting ready to go out to a dinner party with his wife, when his phone rang.

"Hello Matthias, it's Dr Fleischman calling you from the mortuary. Sorry to bother you during the evening, but I've just completed the autopsies on those two males who were brought in from the vehicle crash near Heiligenblut, and the results are rather unusual, so I thought I'd better give you word as soon as possible. My courier will put the full report on your desk later this evening, but I confess I've not seen anything like it before."

"Well, you've certainly got my attention, Fleischman, what is it?"

"Ah, well, you see, they do have the usual sort of injuries you'd expect from a road traffic accident of course, but in addition, they have, what I can only describe as burns, in a kind of slice shape right through parts of their body, including the head."

"Burns! But the vehicle did not catch fire," Schweiger protested.

"And usually," Fleischman continued, "when we see burns, they are to the outer flesh, but these burns go deep through the body."

"So, what would cause burns like that?" Schweiger was suddenly perplexed.

"Well, to be honest, I just don't know," admitted Fleischman. "I think there have been cases when people have been struck by lightning, and the burn has travelled through the body. Or maybe getting in the path of a microwave laser beam or something highly unusual like that?"

"What?... So how old are these burns?" Schweiger was applying his investigative protocol to try to assess the significance of what Fleischman was saying.

"Well they must have been suffered around about the same time as the vehicle crash - the men could not have survived and driven after the burns occurred."

"So you are suggesting that the men suffered the burns, and that caused the crash?"

"Perhaps, but not necessarily," was Fleischman's response. "Alternatively, the crash may have caused something to happen inside the vehicle which then caused the burns. There is no way for me to establish which happened first. Was there any unusual equipment in their vehicle?"

"No, the report only listed hand luggage, blankets - stuff like that. But I will get forensics to double-check in the morning."

"Yes, let me know, will you. I'm intrigued. It's frustrating not being able to pin down the cause."

"And thanks for alerting me this evening, Fleischman, my only witness was due to fly out early tomorrow morning... and this revelation makes me begin to wonder, again, if she was *just* a witness," he added. "This case was already extremely unusual."

After finishing the call with Fleischman, Schweiger pondered for a moment, trying to ignore the shouts from his wife downstairs to hurry up. He decided to call his forensic unit straight away.

"Hello Taube, ja, it's Inspector Schweiger here. Look, something rather important has come up - I wonder if you would mind putting in a couple of hours for me this evening? Firstly, I would like you to go through the luggage of the English couple we have been dealing with, following the Heiligenblut crash. Look for anything in the luggage that might indicate the use of an unusual weapon - fuel, instructions, disguised toiletries - you know what I mean, anything that might cause burns, indeed anything out of the ordinary. Then if you could do the same on the crashed van. Yes, yes, I know you have already reported on the contents of the van, but I am asking you to double-check - again look for any evidence of burns, any unusual equipment. Ja... Ja, danke, Taube, I am grateful."

Schweiger smiled - it was frustrating to not understand what this new information from the autopsy meant, but he had put his best brains on the job. Now he just needed to apply more pressure to the English couple. He was interrupted again by his wife, calling from downstairs.

A few minutes after 19:30, the door of the hospital room opened rather abruptly, and Inspector Schweiger strode in. Kathi had her back to the door, but swung around and jumped to attention. Then she looked at him rather askance - instead of the uniform she was used to, he was dressed in formal evening wear, including a tuxedo. Betty sought to suppress a slight giggle at the incongruity.

"Do you think you should be inside the room, Riegler? You could be taken unawares by an intruder entering," he barked, reacting to her lack of attention and the look on her face.

"I thought... that if I sat outside I would simply be advertising which room our guests are present in, sir?" she replied thoughtfully.

"Mmm... Yes, I suppose so," he concurred generously. "Anyway," he continued, turning to Betty, "it seems that our guests, as you put it, may have been less than completely truthful with me, *again*?" He emphasised the last word and looked questioningly at Betty. She said nothing, appearing confused; and with a slight shake of her head, she opened her palms in a gesture that invited him to be more explicit.

"Ha," he sighed, showing some frustration, "I have just learned the results of the autopsy on those two men who were killed in the crash near Heiligenblut." He paused momentarily, hoping to see a glimmer of recognition in Betty's face, but she still looked blank. "It seems that they were killed before they crashed the van?" He paused again, but Betty simply creased her forehead in bewilderment. "Ha," he sighed again. "By some sort of strange... laser weapon?" he half-shouted, exasperated at the lack of any recognition on Betty's face. Schweiger half-regretted that he had revealed all that he knew. Usually, he would prod a suspect with small pieces of information until they took the bait. But Betty's blank expression made him concerned that perhaps she really did know nothing, and that he was going to struggle to resolve this dilemma.

"Is this some kind of a joke?" Betty asked gently, glancing to Kathi to check how she was reacting to her boss, out of uniform, late evening, and saying bizarre things.

"No," Schweiger responded straight away. "It is never a joke when two men are killed. We have already established that they were a danger to you, and if you confirm to me that you or Mr Tremaine killed them, I am quite open to believing that it was in self-defence. But I need to understand exactly what happened, I can not ignore any of the evidence which comes to me. Tomorrow morning I have the uncle of one of the dead men coming in from Romania to do a formal identification - what the hell am I supposed to tell him?"

Betty was still standing there looking dumbstruck.

"OK... well right now I have an engagement to go to - this has already made me late. Officer Riegler will bring you to my office first thing tomorrow morning, and I hope you will give me satisfactory answers then, *if* you want to be taken to the airport."

He turned and left the room brusquely. He knew that he had used his leverage - they wanted and needed to get home to the UK, and he had implicitly threatened to keep them here until he understood the full sequence of events. But he had an uneasy feeling from Betty's lack of reaction that perhaps she knew nothing about these new facts, and the problem was compounded by his continuing responsibility for her safety whilst she was still in Austria - and moreover, the political pressure which would undoubtedly be put on him to return her to the UK. However, he had played his cards in a timely fashion. He decided to try to put it out of his mind until the following morning, and hurried back down the stairs and out of the hospital entrance, returning to his wife who was waiting impatiently in the car park.

Meanwhile, back in the hospital room, Betty turned to Kathi Riegler to try to make sense of Schweiger's statements. "Does he usually behave like that?" she asked.

"Well, no," confirmed Kathi, sitting back down in one of the chairs. "I've never seen him out of uniform before, but he wasn't drunk if that's what you mean. What he said about the autopsy results must be true, and I think he's a bit agitated because he doesn't yet understand the explanation. He's a very meticulous man - he hates loose ends."

"But it's not fair to detain us here until he can work out the details of what happened," protested Betty.

"Well, look at it from his point of view," suggested Kathi. "You were vulnerable to those abductors, so you were the one to benefit from them being killed, and that makes you the main suspect - you or your protectors. He said he would see it as self-defence," added Kathi.

"Are you suggesting that I should tell him I did it, even though I didn't, so it would set his record straight, and we could go home?" asked Betty.

"Absolutely not," Kathi responded. "I know they use that sort of legal bargaining in the US, but it's certainly not something we would countenance here. No, if you didn't do it, then presumably it must have been UK security agents protecting you?" She glanced questioningly over to George who had been woken by Schweiger's visit, but had as yet said nothing. He simply shook his head slightly, dismissing the idea that he might have been involved. "And he did say," continued Kathi, "that they used some sort of unorthodox weapon - a laser gun I think he said - that suggests security agents to me. The paramedics did mention burn marks that they couldn't explain."

It was at the phrase 'burn marks' that the truth finally hit home to Betty. Her jaw dropped as she experienced the epiphany moment. She rapidly turned away from Kathi to hide her face because it was betraying her realisation. Her expressions were momentarily out of her control, as the implications rushed through her mind. *'So this must be an altered timeline - originally I **was** kidnapped. But... when they found out back at GCHQ, they must have used the i-vector equipment to activate a zap, back in time, to hit the kidnappers near Heiligenblut and prevent the abduction from happening.'* She felt the urge to shout or laugh, but instead was disciplined enough to put together a short act of being distressed, in order to distract Kathi, before asking to be left alone for a while. Kathi obligingly said that she would go and sit outside the room in the corridor for a while, but it was not clear whether she had picked up on Betty's insight.

Betty pulled her chair over to the window and slumped down with elbows on the windowsill to think through the ramifications. This was tricky - not even the management at GCHQ knew about the offensive capability of the i-vector equipment, much less MI5 or MI6 security agents. But Kathi was right - if Betty denied the killings then the spotlight fell squarely on UK security agents. And although Schweiger apparently both had evidence of the killings, and could understand the motive, he did not, indeed he *could* not, have any evidence implicating any individual. But that made it worse - would he continue to hold herself and George in Austria whilst he tried endlessly, but unsuccessfully, to fathom out the perpetrator and the method of the killings? And would there meanwhile be further attempts to kidnap her if she was stuck here, unable to get back to the UK? She felt a shiver of fear - it all seemed so irresolvable. But then a much darker thought came to her. Had the attempt to change the course of time, by eliminating the first kidnappers, failed? Was time itself conspiring to bend the situation back to satisfy its true course of events - that she *should* be kidnapped? Maybe the ultimate course of time was intractable, and refractory to wilful changes by insignificant scientists. Maybe some yet-to-be-understood, dark rule of physics would repeatedly manipulate her situation to prevent her return to the UK, until the danger from the abductors was finally realised in her kidnap? A shiver of fear went through her body. There was only one person with whom she could discuss such grand philosophical physics ideas. She picked up her phone and called Petra.

"Hi Petra, darling, it's Betty, I really need Alex again, sorry." She heard the kids in the background, and then the phone being passed to Alex.

"Hi Betty, are you OK?"

"Well yes," she sobbed slightly at the familiar reassuring sound of Alex's voice, "but things have got a bit complicated, listen." She looked round to check that Kathi was still out of the room and spoke softly. "So, it seems that the kidnappers who were following me, they were mysteriously killed just before they crashed the van, they had burn marks through their body, as if they had been torched by a laser. Think about it Alex. Are you understanding me?"

There were a few seconds of silence on the other end of the phone. "Whoa, OK I follow you. So does that make a difference to your situation?"

"Well, yes, because the Inspector is trying to get his head around 'whodunnit', and since it was apparently done by me, or at least for my benefit, he seems reluctant to let me go until he works it out." Betty glanced round to check the door again.

"Damn, that's tricky, Betty," agreed Alex. "But you absolutely can't tell him."

"I know. But there may be an even scarier issue. I'm wondering if, because… Well, I can't seem to get away from here - every time we prepare to leave, something happens and we find ourselves staying here again - it feels sinister, like a nightmare or a conspiracy. And so I'm beginning to wonder if maybe there is a true course of time, a true course of events, and that if anyone tries to change it, then it just bends back to try to re-establish the original events - so like, in this case, me getting kidnapped is inevitable in the end."

"What! Betty, that's preposterous," objected Alex. "I appreciate you are under a lot of stress at the moment, but you know physics doesn't work like that."

"But we can't know for sure, Alex," protested Betty. "It might seem a bit fanciful but..."

"No Betty, think back to last year, that message that saved us from making a big mistake - that changed the course of events, didn't it?"

"Oh, yes, that's true, I'd forgotten about that. Assuming it was genuine of course. But it was just an advisory message - it wasn't a *direct* attempt to retrospectively change the course of events."

"No, no, you need to stop thinking in that direction, Betty, it's just a distraction. Deal with the real problems. The bottom line is you can't say anything about what we think happened to cause the crash - just stick with 'You didn't do it' and 'You don't know' - which is pretty much true. There is no way they can find any evidence to make you responsible, so ultimately they will have to release you. And you said you are under police protection so you should be safe however long that process takes."

"Well yes, but the police protection is pretty amateurish, we've just got one officer sitting outside the door at the moment. Much as I really like her, I'm not sure she would be a match for any concerted attempt by ruthless hostile agents. I'm seriously wondering if I should just slip away and travel home one way or another. I don't think I can be tracked now - my old phone is switched off, and we no longer have the hired car. Oh, I forgot to tell you, there must have been a tracker on the hire-car, because some woman who was driving in it this afternoon got kidnapped, and then was set free, presumably when they realised it wasn't me."

"Good grief! Look, perhaps I had better come out there to help?" offered Alex.

"No, no, don't do that Alex - it would only complicate things, and you might be in danger too, if you were out here. Stay with the equipment in case we need an intervention, and it also helps me just knowing you are on the end of the phone to talk to."

"Actually, on the end of Petra's phone - security came and took mine away to test - I think they are checking all the annexe peoples' phones after your problem came to light. They said 24 to 48 hours. But what about George? If you try to slip away, is he well enough to go with you?"

"No, he's pretty much out-of-it. The medication they gave him means he's been sleeping most of the day. I *would* feel mean leaving him here, but it does seem to be *me* that's in danger, not him. And there's another issue, Alex - it's not just the police out here who will be scratching their heads about the strange way the would-be abductors were killed. I haven't told MI5 anything yet - but what on earth are they going to think? They *know* they had no one watching my back. They know they didn't do it. And then there is whoever organised the kidnap - they obviously already know our work is valuable, but the manner of this killing would pique their interest even more. I know I ought to feel grateful for the retrospective intervention at Heiligenblut - it undoubtedly saved me from a very nasty experience, but whoever it was that intervened, should have tried to think of a way to cover their tracks better. What a mess."

"I hear what you say, Betty, I'll have a think about that," reflected Alex.

After speaking with Alex, Betty felt a little clearer - at least he had vigorously rejected the dark notion that events were conspiring to make it inevitable that she would be kidnapped, and she generally trusted his judgement.

Kathi looked into the room to say that another officer was taking over from her - Lukas - she called him, "So I am going home now, Betty, but I'll be back at 6 in the morning to drive you..." She tailed off. Clearly, she had wanted to say 'drive you to the airport', but they both realised that the airport was now conditional on first visiting Schweiger's office and satisfying him.

Betty considered phoning Tom Wheatley at MI6. She knew she ought to brief him on Schweiger's interpretation of the autopsy results; otherwise, Tom would be unprepared when Schweiger next spoke to him. But she did not want to get into a discussion with Wheatley about the implications of the autopsy, since the truth needed to be kept from MI5 as well.

But she gathered her resolve and called his number. "Hi Tom," she started, "We are still in the hospital room, but I wanted to bring you up to date on a couple of things. There was an attempted kidnap in Villach this afternoon, and it turns out that the victim was driving the hire-car that George and I were using previously. The woman was freed and is basically OK, I understand. So it seems that our hire-car was definitely being tracked."

"Mmm... that makes sense," agreed Wheatley.

"The other thing is that the autopsy results on the two would-be kidnappers who were killed in the crash near Heiligenblut, suggest that they had strange burns on their bodies - Inspector Schweiger is convinced that they were killed by a laser-gun or something, and that's what caused them to crash. So although the new kidnap attempt has consolidated his view that I am in danger, he is again reluctant to let us leave because he thinks we must know something about the killings."

"What, a laser-gun? That's wacky," remarked Wheatley incredulously.

"Was there," Betty asked ponderously, "an MI6 agent around, watching my back, or something? Oh, Tom, the police officer is coming back. I'll have to end the call now, OK?"

That final question, asking him whether there was an MI6 agent around, was masterful, Betty realised - it implicitly conveyed that she knew nothing about any laser-gun. The idea to phrase it that way had only come to her as she was speaking. But she felt guilty about not being truthful with Tom Wheatley - he had been so reassuring and helpful to her. And she had further lied to him about the police officer returning, in order to break the call and hence avoid any discussion and speculation with him about the fictitious laser-gun.

She took a deep breath and meditated on the situation. She looked over at George - he had dozed off again, undisturbed by her phone calls, during which she had been speaking softly, so as not to be heard by the police officer outside the door. George looked very comfortable and safe. By contrast, she felt trapped. She did not want to spend another day or two or even more, being interrogated by Schweiger, having to lie about what she knew, being bored, endlessly waiting around. And she felt hungry. She had not eaten since the early lunch with Kathi. Hungry and trapped - the answer to both was outside this hospital room - a plan crystallised in her mind. The nurse would be back soon - she came round every hour to do George's observations and update his record. Betty wrote a short note for George, and she guessed ultimately, for the police, explaining why she had skipped out. The guilt came again - it felt horrible leaving George. Guilt was an unaccustomed feeling for Betty - she could chase it away by rationalising that she was being *forced* into leaving and lying by unreasonable circumstances, but the

61

feeling periodically bounced back. She filled up George's glass with water and placed the jug in a strategic position. Whilst she waited for the nurse, she checked again the train times at the railway station, and the route that she would walk to get there. It was only 5 minutes away. Then she put her hair up in a bun, the same way the nurses did here, and waited…

"He's still sleeping." She greeted the nurse with a smile, approaching the bed casually and gestured to George's head. Then as the nurse bent forward to put the blood pressure cuff on George's arm, Betty drew back her arm in an awkward, clumsy move, just as she had rehearsed, and knocked the water jug over, spilling most of its contents over her own top and leggings. It took only seconds then to elicit from the nurse a sympathetic offer to find a set of dry scrubs for Betty to wear while her own clothes dried off. Her amateur dramatic training had made the whole act seem very credible. The nurse hurried out of the room and returned a minute later with the promised scrubs. Though Betty was still acting as distressed by the situation, she was inwardly delighted to see that the scrubs were indeed the same colour as those the nurse was wearing. She set about rapidly changing into the scrubs whilst the nurse started doing George's observations. Betty bundled up her wet clothes. "I'll just wring these out in the bathroom," she informed the nurse, as she crossed to the door, grabbing her coat surreptitiously as she opened the door and left. As she walked out of the door she deliberately turned away from the sitting police officer, hiding the coat and bundle of clothes on her side farthest from him, and then quickly shifting them round to her front as she retreated down the corridor. She had planned and rehearsed the movements, including the way the nurses tended to walk, whilst she had been waiting. The overall intention being that the police officer, if he glanced up, would only see a nurse walking out of the room - he would not see her face or the bundle of clothes. The real nurse had already been in, out, and in again during the last couple of minutes - it seemed unlikely the officer would be clocking ins and outs. In any case, if he did notice and challenge her - the plan B would be simply to say that she had had an accident with the water jug and was going to wring out the clothes in the toilet.

But plan B was not necessary - she simply walked down the corridor, around the corner, slipped on her coat and took the elevator down to the ground floor, where she strode, confidently and nonchalantly, out of the entrance, making for the path that skirted the back of the car park. After the overly warm hospital, the cold quickly made her realise how thin the scrub-leggings were. The bundle of wet clothes began to feel like a liability - she wondered whether to dump them, but she was fond of the outfit and reluctant to forfeit the clothes, so she stopped for a few seconds to wring them out as best she could, the dribbles of water etching pockets into the snow on the path. Then she hurried on, reasoning that she needed to somehow find a bag for the wet clothes, turning into NikolaiStrasse and passing the cafe she had eaten in earlier with Kathi. Gradually the exhilaration of acting-out the hospital exit plan began to fade, and was replaced with some trepidation - it was cold and dark, every passing car or pedestrian could feasibly be a threat. She fingered her phone - she had primed it before leaving. It would zap 5 metres in front of the phone, in the direction the phone was pointing. As a weapon it would realistically only give her one shot - the equipment back in England would take 50 minutes to replenish the energy for another. But more worryingly, it had never been tested - she could only trust that her calculations and calibrations were correct. There would also, she knew, be a pause between pressing the button on the phone, and the equipment projecting the zap - she estimated less than half a second via the carrier signal and Internet, though that was only an educated guess. Still, it was just a short walk to the station and surely then she would be safe, on a train to Zagreb, crossing two country borders in just a few hours, away from Austria, and then a plane flight home.

She turned out of NikolaiStrasse into the road that led to the station. A few more pedestrians on this road. Two men, engaged in conversation, coming toward her - they passed. A woman standing on the other side. A nasty-looking man on a corner eyed her as she passed. She walked on 50 metres and then looked back - he was still there, he hadn't followed. But she noticed another man on the opposite side of the road, running in the same direction she was going, who appeared to glance across at her. Her heart was thumping now, she was feeling some regret at having left the safety of the hospital room. She quickened her pace. The man ran past on the other side, glancing at the phone he held in his hand. The traffic between them, and the piles of cleared snow bordering the road felt like some measure of insulation. He ran on past. Probably late for a train, thought Betty with a smile. But her smile vanished when, as he reached the next pedestrian crossing, after glancing in her direction, he crossed to her side of the road, and walked back toward her. Suddenly she had just seconds to make a decision. There was no side street to duck into. She could carry on walking in the vain hope that he was not actually approaching her. She could turn and run, but then she would not be able to see his movements, and he would undoubtedly catch her up, especially since she was lumbered with the bundle of wet clothes. If she used the weapon she would undoubtedly attract attention, but it might be her only opportunity. Instinctively she backed sideways into an area in front of a cafe, which in the daytime would be filled with tables. It would force him to clarify his intention beyond doubt by turning to approach her, and gave her the few metres of clearance she needed. She readied her phone with a trembling hand, and held it in her pocket, angled forward. The man drew level and turned toward her. "Hello, Betty."

Betty thrust the phone forward in her pocket so that it looked like she was pointing a gun. "Stop right there or I will shoot," Betty growled, surprising herself with the strength of her voice. She judged she would have to fire if he advanced another metre.

"What?" He froze. "Oh, *The snow seems to deaden the shadows here.*"

Betty gasped with realisation and relief, and a little anger. "Oh, you utter twat, I nearly killed you," she spat out. "You scared me to death." Betty stomped forward to where he was standing and thumped him hard on the arm.

"Ow! - Nice to meet you too."

Betty looked into his face for the first time and warmed to him immediately. He was about her age with gingery hair and twinkly eyes. He wore a traditional double-breasted woollen coat, with the collar turned up against the snow, which gave him a well-dressed look. As he made to slip his phone back into his coat pocket, Betty noticed the map with a flashing red dot that presumably had been indicating her location.

"Let's walk on," he said casually, "in case anyone noticed that little charade. I'm from MI6. You can call me Stuart."

"Is that your name?"

"No." He took her by the arm and led her gently along in the direction she had been going. Betty realised that, strangely, she did not mind. "OK, business first. Why are you out here alone? - the update I had from Tom a little while ago was that the police were potentially detaining you for longer?"

"Yeah, I skipped out," answered Betty cryptically.

"Let me guess," he said, studying her appearance. "From the bundle of clothes, and the scrubs, I would say you impersonated a nurse?"

"Right first time," said Betty indifferently, as if she were not impressed; though, in truth, she thought him quite efficient.

"So, do the police know you are gone?" His tone was more serious now.

"I don't know for sure, but I doubt it," she replied. "I just walked past the officer sitting outside our room. He didn't notice *then*..."

"...but the police will inevitably realise at some stage." He verbalised the missing part of her logic. "And where are you going to?"

"Zagreb."

"Why?" His tone communicated incredulity.

"I can ride the train to Zagreb, it's two countries away, and then get a flight back to the UK."

"Oh dear."

"Oh dear, what?"

"Well, yes, you'll have no trouble crossing the borders to Zagreb because it's still within the EU - no passports," reasoned Stuart, "but as soon as you try to check-in for an international flight with your passport, you will be arrested by the Zagreb airport police, who will have been notified of a European Arrest Warrant from the Villach police. The police here won't just let you 'skip-out'. And then you get to come back to Villach to spend more time with the cops, who are now even more grouchy because you tricked them."

"But the cops may not have realised I'm gone by the time I get to Zagreb - It's only 4 or 5 hours," protested Betty hopefully.

"By the time you check-in for a UK flight it will be more like lunchtime tomorrow," retorted Stuart authoritatively.

"All right clever-dick, where should I go then?" Betty was holding back tears - her plan had been crushed.

"Well... I could drive you to a beach on the French coast near Calais, where we could get you whisked across the channel by a clandestine boat. But it's a 13-hour drive - you wouldn't like that."

"Try me."

"Where's your luggage?"

"It's still at the police station, but I don't care about that."

"Ah then, unfortunately, I am not allowed to. You see our UK people are desperate to get back your old phone so they can analyse it to understand how it was hacked. That's almost as important to them as you are. You see, if lots of phones have been hacked somehow, there is big trouble, beyond just you getting nearly abducted. So we have to keep the Austrian police sweet, so they will do us the favour of letting us have that phone."

"But…"

"And on top of that, our UK people are desperate to get sight of those other photos of yourself that the police found on those unfortunate would-be abductors, because those photos hold clues as to how they identified you, and how they built this whole scam. And the photos might hold clues about how they have identified other critical personnel at GCHQ. So, it's the bigger picture, you see. We have to keep friendly with the Austrian police so we can get those items of evidence from them."

"So you're saying I should go back to the hospital?" protested Betty incredulously.

Stuart stopped walking. He looked into Betty's eyes for a moment, and just nodded. The look on his face was of sympathy, and it belied his previous playful attitude in conversation - it was clear he knew that this would be an emotionally difficult thing for Betty to do.

"Think of it as your patriotic duty?" suggested Stuart.

"No, I can't - you don't know all the angles," protested Betty.

"Oh? What don't I know about?" asked Stuart, looking into her face intently. Betty realised she was being pushed onto sticky ground.

"Well, I'm very hungry, for one thing." The perfect answer - it was truthful but diversionary.

"Ah, well that's something I *can* help you with," quipped Stuart, apparently pleased that he could actually help in some way. "Let me just check a couple of things." He pulled his phone from his pocket. "OK, the police apparently are still unaware you are missing - there is no bulletin out on you, as yet." He studied the map. "This way." He lifted the bundle of wet clothes out of her grasp and guided her quickly round a corner, away from the railway station.

"So you are monitoring police communications as well?" deduced Betty.

"Yes, it's a very useful tool sometimes. *They* wouldn't like it of course - not strictly legal. But it means we should be able to risk the time for a meal - a quick one." They turned another couple of corners, and Stuart led her into an entrance with the sign 'Waschsalon'. Before she had fully realised where they were, he had tossed the bundle of wet clothes into a dryer and inserted coins into the slot to start it. Betty couldn't help but smile at his sheer efficiency. They left the launderette and crossed the road to a restaurant. Stuart didn't wait for the menus but talked to the waiter briefly in a stream of German, which Betty didn't manage to translate, though she assumed he had asked for food to be brought without a delay. The waiter hurried off.

"Hang on, what have you ordered?" complained Betty.

"Goulash."

"And what if I don't like it?"

"Everybody loves goulash."

"But maybe I'm a vegetarian?" posited Betty.

"You're not - I've read your personnel file," he countered. Betty sighed resignedly. He sat her down in a booth away from other diners, and positioned himself opposite her, so that he was facing the door.

"Anyway," he continued in a hushed tone, "importantly, goulash comes straight out of the pot, so we won't have to wait. And, for your information, I had just, myself, started eating when your red dot began moving on my screen map, announcing your untimely escapade. So, I had to abort my meal and run to find you. That means I'm hungry too. But here's a menu - you can choose your own dessert, we'll order it now and the waiter can line it up. He glanced at his phone again checking the police bulletins."

The waiter arrived after a couple of minutes with steaming bowls of deep reddish-brown goulash, and took their orders for drinks and desserts. They both gave all their attention to the food. Betty could not believe how good the goulash tasted. There was silence for a couple of minutes.

"How's the goulash?" asked Stuart at length.

"Oh, It's OK," begrudged Betty.

Stuart looked disappointed. "Right, so when you threatened to shoot me earlier," continued Stuart quietly, "have you actually got a weapon in your pocket or were you just acting?"

"No I haven't got a gun in my pocket," Betty replied flatly, avoiding the complexity of the question. "As you probably heard from

Tom, I temporarily acquired a Soviet Makarov from the kidnappers, but the police confiscated it from me before I could try it out on anyone." That made Stuart laugh.

"What about *you*," Betty continued, parodying polite transactional conversation, "have you got a gun in *your* pocket?"

"Yes, actually." He took another mouthful of food. "So when Tom last briefed me, he said that Inspector Schweiger had some strange new theory about the kidnappers being killed by a laser-gun? Can you tell me more about that?"

Betty thoughtfully chewed on a piece of meat. "Well, there's not much more to tell. Apparently, the autopsy stated that the kidnappers were killed before the crash. They had burn marks - Schweiger concluded they had been killed by a laser-gun. The problem is that Schweiger concludes, actually not unreasonably, that it must have been done by my guardian angel or myself... It wasn't you was it?" Betty was half-heartedly trying the implicit denial technique on Stuart, but she doubted it would work on a man so clearly sharp.

Stuart laughed. "No, they don't issue us with laser-weapons. Though if they did I would have been happy to use it on those bastards, in a romantic gesture to save you."

The use of the word 'romantic' caught Betty's attention, and she looked up at Stuart to try to understand where he was coming from.

"What about *you*," Stuart mimicked her phrase of earlier, "do they issue *you* with laser-guns?" He had thrown the question at her whilst she had been looking directly at him, making it much more difficult to lie. She took a second before answering, but did not avert her gaze.

"No, of course they don't, Stuart. We are development scientists, not secret agents."

"I don't think you are being completely truthful with me," observed Stuart.

"No, you're right. - The goulash was incomparably delicious."

Stuart smiled. "OK, but if you don't tell us everything, then it makes it very difficult for us to help you, and to satisfy Schweiger, and to get the evidence from him, that we need."

"Yes, I am well aware of that. I have told you all I can. I work in a top-secret area, I am not legally allowed to say anything to you or anyone else about it, even if I thought it was helpful. Just like you won't even tell me your real name, Mister not-Stuart. However, I *can* tell you truthfully that I did not kill the kidnappers. I knew nothing about them until I saw the aftermath of their crash on the mountain. Therefore, fortunately, there is no way the police can find any evidence against me, or my colleague, George, in that respect. So I suggest you work from that basis - the rest is up to you. Unfortunately, I suppose the next candidate for Schweiger's suspicion would be an over-protective secret agent - in fact, someone rather like yourself, Stuart. So I suggest you keep your head down otherwise you might get detained by the police as well."

Stuart nodded and smiled.

"Apparently," she continued, "Schweiger is a meticulous man and gets agitated if there are loose ends - he seemed to be worried about what he should say to the uncle of one of the dead men who is coming tomorrow, to identify his nephew."

"An uncle?" Stuart suddenly looked serious.

"What? Oh, you think he might be an accomplice rather than an uncle?" deduced Betty.

"It seems likely, we already know that there were two more of them around earlier today, pulling that other kidnap stunt. But it's not good news when they have access to the police - I wonder if Schweiger realises that possibility?" mused Stuart.

"Schweiger is an intelligent man," Betty assured him.

"Yes, but I'll get Tom Wheatley to phone him tomorrow morning to make sure he is aware of the possibility of a hostile impostor. Right. So, your colleague, George - he is recovering in the hospital from a concussion? How did that happen?"

"It's completely unrelated to anything, Stuart. He slipped over, walking back to find me, when we got separated in the blizzard yesterday."

"And are you completely sure that he had nothing to do with foiling the original kidnap attempt?"

Betty laughed. "George is not exactly action-man. He was asleep when I left him, and still asleep when I got back after the failed kidnap. Come to think of it, he's been asleep most of today as well - although to be fair, that's because of the medication."

"So why did you leave him alone when you left the ski resort -

had you had an argument?"

"Well, oh, you're pushing me into another area which I don't want to talk about because it's very personal. But no, we hadn't had an argument. It was nothing to do with him, it was to do with my health." She noticed Stuart suddenly avert his eyes. "Oh, what, so you've read my personnel file and you know about my impending health issue?"

Stuart nodded pityingly.

"Please don't look at me like that, Stuart. OK, so if you know, I may as well explain, but please don't say anything in front of George - I haven't told him about it yet, I need to find a good time. So, you see, just recently, the Huntington's involuntary movements have started - in fact, that's how I spun the car yesterday and lost George temporarily. But I have known this was coming for years so I am well prepared mentally. I had decided to leave the ski resort, alone, early that morning to head for Switzerland, where I could have a dignified assisted suicide. But ironically, after all the emotional difficulty of settling on that decision, events have rather trashed my intended path." Betty's voice cracked on the final words and she sniffed to avoid losing composure. Stuart reached across the table and squeezed her free hand gently and sympathetically. Betty's other hand held the fork with which she was eating her apple strudel dessert. She was dimly aware that in other circumstances, she might have stabbed his hand with the fork, but, unusually, she liked the way this man behaved, and she did indeed feel genuinely comforted by his touch. She ate the last mouthfuls of strudel in a sullen silence without pulling her hand away from his.

A couple had just walked into the restaurant. Because of the high back to the booth, Betty could not see them until they walked past. As she glanced up she realised that the woman was Kathi Riegler, who fortunately had not yet looked over in her direction. Betty's heart thumped. She tightened her hand around Stuart's and pulling him close whispered, "A policewoman just walked in - get me out of here quickly."

Stuart calmly rose from his seat, dropped some Euro notes on the table, and pulled Betty up out of her seat, very close to himself so that his large frame shielded her from view. To Betty, it felt like she was being led in ballroom dancing. She just allowed herself to walk, keeping a close physical connection to him, accepting the firm and steady gentle insistence from his torso, as he loudly thanked the waiter and guided her out of the door, shielding her the whole time. As they hurriedly crossed the road to the launderette, Betty kept hold of Stuart's hand and he kept his arm around her. It took them only a matter of half a minute to remove the almost-dried clothes from the drier, bundle them up and quickly head off along the road again.

Betty felt her brief panic giving way to exhilaration. "God, that was close, you were brilliant Stuart, how do you keep so calm and do everything so smoothly and effortlessly?"

"Oh, it's just a frame of mind - we are trained to always be ready for the unexpected, and so I had already thought through most scenarios in my head, in preparation. Anyway, back to the hospital now?"

"OK." Betty agreed meekly, but had mixed feelings. She was beginning to really enjoy this time and excitement with Stuart, but she also wanted to be back in the relative safety and quiet of the hospital room. The food had lifted her spirits, and she was more confident that the period of police detention would not be too much longer, after talking it through with Stuart. It also helped knowing that there were UK people safeguarding her interests.

"One other question," said Stuart, as they walked briskly back in the direction of the hospital. "When you first realised who I was, after first insulting me, you said that you had nearly killed me. And it seemed at the time like you really meant it. But if you haven't a gun or a laser in your pocket, how would you have nearly killed me?"

Betty threw back her head and laughed. She was in no mood to be pulled into sticky water by Stuart's genuinely profound psychological analysis; she would save her serious answers for Schweiger. "I'm a witch, Stuart, I would have called on my guardian angel to strike you down with a bolt of lightning." Stuart looked *be*mused rather than *a*mused, and Betty wondered if her metaphor had been a bit too close to reality anyway. They walked on.

As they neared the hospital, Stuart stopped. "I'll let you walk the last part on your own, just in case there is anyone watching - I need to stay invisible if possible."

"Oh." Betty could not help sounding disappointed. "I've really enjoyed this time with you Stuart." She reached up and kissed him, then grabbed her clothes bundle from him and made off toward the hospital entrance.

Stuart was left sadly wondering if he would ever see her again. Then he phoned Tom Wheatley and briefed him on everything that had happened, and everything he had learned from Betty.

"I don't like the sound of this autopsy/burn-marks/laser-gun nonsense," mused Wheatley. "What the hell is going on? I suppose I can ask for a copy of the autopsy from Schweiger tomorrow - maybe we'll understand better then, unless the whole thing is a ruse to keep them there longer."

"I don't think so," voiced Stuart. " I got the impression that Betty knows what happened, but she won't open up about it. When I first caught up with her, she was terrified I was a kidnapper, and then, when she realised who I actually was, she said she had almost killed *me* - I'm sure she meant it. But I had my arm round her a couple of times and I could feel no weapon in her pockets. Fortunately, she thinks very fast and I doubt the police will trip her up - she seems convinced that there is no way they could find evidence against her. Do we have any idea what she was working on back at GCHQ - are there any clues there?"

"No," said Wheatley. "I asked her boss and he just said she was working on a new method of surveillance - he wouldn't elucidate, but he assured me it had nothing to do with weapons."

"I'm wondering," mused Stuart, "if maybe I should sneak into the police compound, and try to slip something into the kidnappers crashed van that looks like it might have caused the burns - a taser or flame-thrower or something. That would make it look like the burns had been self-inflicted?"

"Nice thought," agreed Wheatley, "but we don't know the nature of the burns yet. If we get it wrong, it will look really suspicious. And they may have already done forensics on the van - if a flame thrower suddenly turns up it will seem too obvious that it has been planted. No, just stay in protective mode for the moment. I don't like the sound of this **Romanian uncle either** - see if any of your contacts have any information on hostile agent movements."

Chapter 5
A Fateful Phone call

Stefan Taube, although he had mildly protested to Schweiger about being asked to go back into the police station, loved his forensic work, especially when it involved something out of the ordinary. Just this afternoon he had located a tracking device in the wheel-arch of a hired car, and had lifted a partial fingerprint from it. True, it had only matched with one of the dead men from the Heiligenblut crash, as had been expected, but it was a satisfying forensic linkage. Then he had spent a bit of time partially dismantling the tracking device to see how it was constructed, and written a report on that.

Thus, he was in an enthusiastic mood as he pulled the two luggage cases of the English couple out of the locker where they had been stashed, and emptied out the contents of one of them onto his large working table. His gaze immediately fell on a small object wrapped in aluminium foil. He smiled with anticipation, but decided to dispense with the other items first. He checked the case for any other compartments, but found no further items. He then worked through Betty's clothes, putting each garment aside as he found nothing unusual, and then went through her toilet bag, scanning and checking the contents of any containers. There was absolutely nothing unusual. And so, with relish, he finally moved onto the object wrapped in aluminium foil. First, he scanned it - the scan picture revealed what looked like a regular cell phone. He carefully peeled away the aluminium foil. It certainly did appear to be a regular phone, but why wrap it in aluminium foil if it was simply that? Rather than switch it on, in case that might be activating some sort of weapon, he decided to remove the back cover to look inside. But again, it still had all the appearance of an orthodox phone. So, he carefully pressed the on-button to establish whether it actually functioned as a phone. Sure enough, it appeared to boot-up and presented a home screen. He decided to use it to try calling his own phone, to finally validate its function, and was very disappointed to find that it did, indeed, successfully call him. Rather despondently, he returned everything to the luggage case, except the phone, which he pushed aside, intending to examine it further later on.

Methodically he now emptied the contents of the second case onto his large table, and immediately noted with some exasperation another similar item wrapped in aluminium foil. But he started working rigorously through the contents, as his thoughts now turned to the van - perhaps he would find something more interesting in that.

*   *   *

Maxim Kuznetsov was, by contrast, thoroughly despondent. The three months that he had spent monitoring the English woman and planning, had come to nothing - the Romanian idiots had failed to achieve the initial intercept which had somehow resulted in them killing themselves. And the hurriedly arranged second attempt had revealed that the English woman no longer had the hired car - presumably she had left Austria. And he was unclear whether any of his agents' activities had alerted the UK people or not. Kuznetsov had drunk his way through a third of a bottle of whiskey that he thought was well deserved to compensate him for his wasted efforts. He was slumped in an armchair contemplating his woes. At the precise moment that Stefan Taube had ended his test call on Betty's phone, Kuznetsov's laptop computer started bleeping - not the dull bleep of an arriving email but the continuing lighter bleep of his tracking software. This was unexpected - he had already discontinued monitoring the useless tracker on the hire-car, and the Englishwoman's phone itself had been turned off for two days. He tried to spring up from the armchair, and staggered slightly, belatedly regretting that he had drunk so much. But maybe now he would at least know for sure that she was back in the UK, and her calls and messages, that the software would relay to him, might give him some idea whether she was aware of the abduction plan or not. He banged his knee against the leg of the table sitting down, and cursed that he had started on the whiskey so early in the evening. But as he focussed on the map displayed on the laptop screen, he was surprised and excited to find that the location of the flashing dot was still Austria. He zoomed in on the map - still in Villach, he zoomed in farther to identify the building - it seemed to be part of the police headquarters. What did this mean? He sat back in the chair and tried to think. He knew from her phone message the day before that she was heading for Salzburg. She had detoured to Villach and was in some way involved with the police - it pointed strongly to her having been involved in an accident with the Romanians' van. Perhaps she had been injured. After all, the Romanian men had died in the accident. Perhaps the police had driven her car back to Villach and they had returned it to the hire company. But that didn't make sense - the car must have been damaged in any crash and surely would not have been repaired and re-hired so quickly. And why had the phone been turned off for two days? - Uncharacteristic for her. He needed to be sure that she was still in possession of the phone; otherwise, he was wasting his time again. On a whim, he dialled her number - if her voice answered then he would be sure, and he could just hang up.

Stefan Taube was working his way through George's toiletries when Betty's phone, which he had placed at the end of the table, rang. He picked it up and looked at the screen, which showed a cell phone number rather than a caller's name. At first, he hesitated whether to answer it or not - it was always so awkward when answering someone else's phone - it was usually friends or relatives who got worried and panicked when they found out it was being answered by the police. And he was working alone tonight - no one else to hand the phone to if his skills at reassurance proved inadequate. Then he remembered that this whole case was full of intrigue and interest, so he swiped the screen and answered, without formally stating his name first, as he normally would. "Guten Tag."

Kuznetsov heard the male voice, and his heart initially sank, but then he thought it would be useful to wing it, to try to get more information. "Oh, Guten Tag, I was expecting to speak with Betty - is she not there?" Kuznetsov cursed himself as he realised the slight drawl in his own voice, and the alcohol taking some toll on his efforts at an English accent.

"Who is this please?" inquired Taube.

"Oh, this is her... father, I have been trying to reach her for a couple of days, but her phone has been off - I am a bit worried - who are you please?" He wondered if he was over-compensating the English accent, but suspected that a German speaker would not be able to discern the difference.

Taube hesitated - the call had come in as an unidentified number, and that was inconsistent with this caller being her father, whose number would almost certainly be identified by her phone's contact list. "Ah, OK sir, this is the police - there is nothing to worry about, but we are looking after your daughter's luggage temporarily. I will pass a message to her that you wish to speak with her."

"Oh, my goodness, what has happened to her?" Kuznetsov inwardly winced at his awful over-dramatised attempt at English.

"I am afraid I can not give you any further information over the telephone sir - but, as I said, I will let her know you phoned, or if you would like to phone the Inspector tomorrow morning?" Taube was needing to cover all bases - be polite and reassuring in case this really was a relative, but giving out no information in case it was not.

"Has she had an accident? Is she OK?" persisted the concerned father-impostor Kuznetsov.

"I promise you there is nothing to be concerned about sir, now if you will forgive me I have another urgent call to attend to, goodbye sir." Taube was reasonably sure that he was being pressurised, and was fairly proud of the competent way he had firmly and politely dispatched the caller. So he immediately rang forensic headquarters in Vienna and requested them to trace the caller's number.

Using his current phone was a mistake Kuznetsov would not have made if he had been sober. Indeed the next morning, when he would awake with a hangover, he would have a nagging feeling at the back of his mind that he should change his phone. But he would dismiss that feeling, remembering that he had already done so the previous day.

*   *   *

Vienna phoned Taube back a few minutes later, and told him that the call had originated from a cell phone in Constanţa in Romania. He punched the air in triumph at the connection, and wondered whether to call Schweiger. But then he decided that he would first specifically rule out the possibility that the caller really had been the English woman's father. He phoned Kathi Riegler, whom he knew had been guarding her, though he did not know where.

"Hi Kathi, it's Stefan Taube. I wondered if you could check something with the Englishwoman for me. A call came in on her phone, and the caller was claiming to be her father. But when I traced the call I found it originated in Romania. Could you ask her if there is any possibility her father is in Romania on business or holiday or some such? I just want to be certain that the number is actually connected with the kidnappers before I tell Schweiger."

"Oh, Stefan, I would, but I am not with her at the moment - I am off-duty for a few hours. Lukas is guarding her room but I don't have his number, and you had best not ask over the radio. Why don't you pop down there and ask her yourself - she's in the hospital, room 607."

"OK, thanks, Kathi." Taube decided he would drop into the hospital on his way home.

*   *   *

Kuznetsov sank back in his armchair with another whiskey to analyse what had been said, and not said, in the call and what information that implied. The police have her luggage, so wherever she is, it is not just a regular hotel-room stay. The police officer had suggested that she would be able to phone him back. That made it sound like she is not in custody. Where else would she not be able to keep her luggage with her - ah, maybe the hospital - maybe she had been injured in the interaction with the Romanians' van after all. And the officer had said there was nothing to be concerned about, so presumably, it was not a serious injury. So, she might not be there long. Ah, there was some hope after all. He felt some optimism return. He would put his agents on to it. After this afternoon's kidnap fiasco they had changed vehicles twice, and withdrawn to a hotel room in Kellerberg, a few miles outside Villach. They would not be pleased with another drive back into Villach. He laughed - that would serve them right. Ah no, he remembered it had not actually been their fault, his logic was addled by the alcohol. Yes - a vigil in the hospital car park, maybe one of them could poke around inside the hospital for information. That would be safer than a vigil outside the police headquarters - he laughed again. He knew it would be no use phoning the hospital - they would never give out patient information over the phone. He wondered if his thinking was simplistic and over-optimistic? No, he thought, it was worth a try, even if his deductions were probabilities rather than facts. He phoned his two agents and put them back on the road. Now, there was another notification on his laptop screen - two monitored messages from the Englishwoman's phone. Ah, more information he thought gleefully. But the first was an unanswered call, and the second was, of course, his own call, embarrassingly playing back his ham attempts at sounding like an English gentleman. Kuznetsov cursed and retreated back to his armchair and whiskey. But maybe this time he would get lucky, he mused. And if not, he still had one other string to his bow.

It was now around nine in the evening as Betty strode back in through the hospital entrance, and took the elevator up to their floor. She was not sure how the police officer, who was stationed outside their door, would react to her arrival. Presumably, according to Stuart, he was still unaware of her departure. She remembered Kathi had said his name was Lukas, and Betty rehearsed as many exchanges as she could imagine as the lift went up. She was not even sure if he knew what she looked like. It would probably be best not to try to impersonate a nurse again, she thought, as she walked confidently up to their door. Lukas looked up. "Wo ist dein Ausweis?" he asked, standing up.

Betty stumbled on the translation. "Where is my, what... oh, identity badge," she realised. "No, Lukas, look it's me, Fräulein Gosmore, whom you are guarding."

"Ha! where...?"

"I just popped down for some food and to dry some clothes that were wet." She held up the bundle of clothes as if by way of explanation, and walked past him into the room. He followed her in, looking around the room carefully to satisfy himself that it was indeed only her and George who were there now.

"You should have asked me," he castigated.

"Oh, sorry," Betty apologised meekly. She let her hair back down and smiled innocently at him. He looked at her again, and muttered something to himself in German as he left the room. She felt slightly regretful that she had probably made him feel inadequate, but her overriding feeling was of adventure fulfilled.

George stirred. "Where have you been?" he yawned.

"Oh, I just went to get some food," she assured him. Then she added rather wistfully, "... Goulash and apple strudel." She hung the almost-dry clothes over the radiators, and pulled the cushions off the chairs to make a bed on the floor, since the hospital had declined Kathi's request to find another bed for the room. She decided she would read another couple of chapters before settling down and going to sleep.

*   *   *

It took Kuznetsov's agents less than half an hour to drive back into Villach and park up in the hospital car park with a good view of the entrance. They had been less than impressed by Kuznetsov's accuracy earlier in the day, when they had found the woman driving the tracked car was not, in fact, their Englishwoman target. And they were uneasy about Kuznetsov's statement that it was only a probability that the Englishwoman was staying in the hospital, especially since he had sounded drunk in the phone call. But Felix and Jakob were professionals, and they accepted that the job was not always straightforward or easy...

*   *   *

Stefan Taube had finished re-examining the crashed van, as Schweiger had requested. Taube had already previously done a basic forensic examination when the vehicle had first arrived, and he found nothing new, but he intended to point out to Schweiger that his original report had noted burns to the men's clothing. Though he had found nothing that might be the cause of the burns. Somewhat disappointed, he drove from police headquarters the short distance to the hospital looking forward to a short interview with the mysterious Englishwoman, whom he had not yet met face to face.

Jakob nudged his colleague. A van marked 'Büro für Kriminaltechnik' (Forensic Science) had just swung into the car park. "Kuznetsov said that the police were holding the woman's luggage, it is possible that the police are paying her a visit. I will follow him in to see if we can get any leads." Jakob slipped quietly out of their vehicle and followed Taube toward the hospital entrance, a respectful distance behind. Through the entrance, he saw Taube heading for the elevator and quickened his pace so that he could join him. Taube, unsuspecting, politely held the door open for him.

"Ah, Danke." Jakob was all smiles. "Do you think it will snow some more tonight?" he asked, conversationally breaking the ice.

"The forecast says not," replied Taube, pressing the button for the sixth floor and glancing at Jakob questioningly.

"Six, ah yes, danke," replied Jakob with practised ease. "I think it is maybe a little colder tonight?"

"Minus five degrees, I believe," responded Taube who was more comfortable with scientific notation than anecdote or opinion. He unzipped his jacket in response to the imposing warmth of the hospital interior. The elevator reached the sixth floor and the doors opened.

Jakob gestured naturally with his arm for Taube to step out first. Taube saw the sign opposite, directing him to turn left for rooms 603 - 615 and did so. Jakob demonstratively turned the other way and said goodnight. Then Jakob glanced back to see Taube turn left again, at which point he silently ran to where Taube had turned, and listened intently.

As Taube had rounded the corner he had seen Lukas sitting in a chair outside room 607 looking thoroughly bored. "Hey Lukas, how are things?"

"Oh, hello Taube, what are you doing here?"

"I need to ask the Englishwoman a question to confirm a piece of evidence before I report it to Schweiger," replied Taube approaching the door.

Lukas stood up. "I envy you, Taube, - your job is so much more interesting than mine." He opened the door to introduce Taube. Betty looked up from her reclined position on the cushions where she was reading. "Fraulein Gosmore, this is officer Taube from Forensics - he would like to ask you some questions, please." Lukas then left the room to sit outside again.

Betty stretched and smiled up at Taube.

"Did they not supply you with a proper bed?" asked Taube surprised.

"It doesn't matter, for just one night," responded Betty. She lifted the cushions from the floor and threw them onto the two chairs gesturing Taube to sit down, and sitting down herself in the other chair. "So, forensics," she continued, "that must be a fascinating job?"

"Yes, it is," he replied, appreciating the expression of interest.

"I'm a sort of scientist myself," added Betty, by way of explanation.

Taube nodded.

Betty stretched. "So what did you want to ask me about?"

"Well, just one question really," started Taube. "Is there any possibility that your father is on holiday, or on business in Romania at the moment?"

"Uh... what?" Betty's whole posture changed at the mention of her father, her eyes welled with tears, and her voice cracked slightly. "Why on earth would you ask a question like that?" She looked away and bit her lip as difficult memories erupted.

"Oh, I'm sorry." Taube was uncomfortable with the effect his question had had on the Englishwoman. "Well, to explain, you see, I took a call on your phone whilst I was checking through your luggage…"

Betty's mouth opened wide. "Why the hell were you going through my luggage?" she snapped. "Oh, I know… you were searching for Schweiger's fantasy laser-gun, I suppose. Well did you find it?"

"No, no… Please let me explain." Taube was concerned that his personal skills were apparently proving inadequate yet again. "Yes, Inspector Schweiger instructed me to check your luggage to rule out any weapons - he is duty-bound to cover all the possibilities. But whilst I was doing that, your phone rang and I answered it. The caller said that he was your father and that he was concerned that he had not been able to contact you for a couple of days. I told him not to worry and that I would pass on the message to you. But I was suspicious about the call, so I asked Federal Forensics to trace the call, and they confirmed that it had originated in Constanţa, Romania. So I came to ask you that question about your father so we can clarify whether the call was genuine or not."

"Oh, I see…" Betty immediately understood the unstated implication, and regained her composure. "I'm sorry, Officer… Taube? Was it? I should not have snapped at you. Show me the number."

"Why do you want to see the number?" Taube was surprised.

"So I can see if I recognise it of course," retorted Betty rather sharply, anticipating that it would put Taube on the back foot again.

"Oh, OK." It sounded reasonable to Taube, put like that, and he wanted to regain her cooperation. He reached into his trouser pocket and pulled out his notebook. He turned to the most recent page and held it up to Betty, pointing at the number.

She was silent for a couple of seconds. "No, I don't recognise it. Actually, my father died about 15 years ago, that's why your question upset me."

"Oh, I'm sorry," answered Taube. In his mind, he wanted to know why she had asked to see the number if the call had so obviously not been from her father, but he thought it unwise to potentially rile this lady further. He had no idea that Betty had just memorised the number.

"So," continued Betty, "now you have another clue to the kidnappers - I understand their van came from Romania?"

"Yes, indeed, it should help with the enquiries." Taube was startled at how quickly the woman had drawn the conclusion. "Well, that was all I wanted to ask. I will leave now and let you rest. Have a good evening. I'm sorry I upset you." He walked to the door. Then he turned to face her again. "Actually I do have one other question. Why did you wrap your phones in aluminium foil?"

"We think the kidnappers were possibly tracking my phone. The metal foil would block the signal."

"But why not just leave it turned off?" he asked, still puzzled.

"Because if the tracking device had its own battery, just turning the phone off would not fix the problem," explained Betty.

"Ha," Taube nodded, smiled, and left. He was impressed with the thoroughness of the thinking - these people were extremely interesting. He said goodnight to Lukas, made his way back down in the elevator, out to the car park, and drove home.

*   *   *

Jakob had heard the exchange between Taube and Lukas mentioning the Englishwoman, and he had heard Lukas introduce Taube to 'Fraulein Gosmore' whilst the door had been open, but he had not been able to hear any more, once Lukas had closed the door and resumed his vigil outside. However, there was really no need for him to push his luck any further - he now knew she was there, he knew the approximate room number, and he knew that there was a police officer stationed right outside the door. He had also noticed that the next floor up in the elevator was labelled 'Helipad' and had taken the elevator up to have a quick look. Then he had returned to Felix outside in the van to talk through their options and possibilities.

*   *   *

As soon as Taube left, Betty phoned Tom Wheatley at MI5 - she felt she would have preferred to phone Stuart, but she had no contact number for him. "Hi, Tom. it's Betty again - I have some information for you." She repeated the story as Taube had told her, and gave him the phone number. "I don't think I mentioned earlier - the police told us that the crashed van was registered in Romania, so that ties in with the phone number - presumably the organiser of the kidnap, do you think?"

"Ah, the Black Sea Gateway," said Tom. "Yes, that seems very likely. Thanks, Betty - that number is very useful."

"So will you be able to trace his location through that number?"

"Well it's possible, but unlikely," said Tom. "Most agents would ditch a phone, or at least ditch the SIM card containing that number, if they realise there is any possibility of being tracked. But the meta-data from using the phone will still be on the network carrier, so we may be able to pull other numbers that he has been in contact with over the last few days - your GCHQ people are the experts in that - I'm just keying in a request to them for analysis on that number right now. It's all useful in building a bigger picture."

"Oh," Betty was disappointed to hear that the phone might already be ditched, but another idea was forming in her mind. "So what sort of phones do agents use - do they use cheap ones because they are likely to be thrown away so quickly? Or do they use the more expensive ones with the best capabilities?"

"That's a strange question," retorted Tom laughing.

"Humour me," requested Betty.

"Well, we wouldn't normally try to economise on things like mobile phones - we want agents to have the best tools available, and their phone is a minuscule part of our budget in keeping them operational. But I can't be sure how the other side works. Why are you asking?"

"Oh, just idle curiosity," replied Betty noncommittally.

"So, I gather you met our, um, Stuart this evening?" remarked Tom.

"Oh, yes, he seems like a really capable guy." Betty was surprised at the enthusiasm in her own voice.

"Yes, he is there to look after you, but please don't go on any more wanders without talking it through with me first, it could put you in a lot of danger." Betty pouted as Wheatley spoke, sounding like a school headmaster talking to a naughty pupil.

"Ah," he continued, "so the GCHQ metrics have just come back to me - that phone is still switched on, and in Constanţa, though we can't be sure whether it is still with the owner of course. And I have three recent contact numbers from it that I can put traces on as well - I suppose one of them will be your old phone that the forensic officer answered. Can you tell me the number of that phone of yours so that I can eliminate it from the list?" Betty recited it to him. "Umm, yes - that's the penultimate call. Right. I'd better get on to this straight away, Betty. We may be able to find those jokers who tried the kidnap this afternoon, and see if they are still in the area. Thanks for this information Betty - ring me anytime."

The door opened and the nurse breezed in again to do her hourly 'obs' on George. "Are your clothes drying out nicely?" she asked brightly.

"Oh, yes fine thanks." Betty felt a glimmer of guilt for having tricked and used her.

"Well, we've taken your friend off his medication now, ready for the morning," she continued, going through the motions of taking his blood pressure yet again. "So he should be a bit more awake soon. It must be a bit boring for you when he's just sleeping most of the time?" Betty smiled - it had almost seemed like George hadn't been there most of the day.

Betty thought over what Tom had said. The 'penultimate' call - that meant the troll in Romania, whoever he was, had made a call *after* speaking with Taube - she felt a pang of worry - had Taube inadvertently revealed any information about where she was? It seemed unlikely - Taube was a professional. She had a police officer sitting outside, and her phone weapon in her pocket. And now, this knowledge of the Romanian phone number had planted a new idea in her head about how to enhance the capabilities of her 'phone weapon'.

At present, she could project a zap accurately, but only close to her own phone. However, during a phone call, if she could get her phone to auto-query the GPS coordinates of the other party's phone, then their GPS location could be used to direct a zap.

But many phones still had inaccurate GPS chips - she could not just send a zap on the off chance that it would find its target - it might just hit some innocent nearby. That was the reason she had queried Wheatley about whether agents would be likely to have the latest phones - it seemed likely they did, from what he had said. So, she now realised, by programming her own phone to auto-query, using IMEI, which GPS chip-set the caller's phone was using, she could establish for certain if that caller's phone had an accurate GPS location or not.

And, if their phone had accurate GPS, then she would be able to zap the person on the other end of the phone. That would make a very formidable weapon.

Betty smiled - more for the sheer ingenuity of the idea, than in any malice. She sat for a while, querying and studying information from the Internet about GPS chips and phone APIs, then started coding logic into her phone. It was extremely tedious on the small screen - she wished she could go down to the Internet cafe, and use a proper computer. But there was no real chance of getting past Lukas again, and the cafe would probably be shut by now anyway. So, she persevered, constructing the intricate code with increasing satisfaction and excitement, but also with aching thumbs and eyes. Finally, after two hours of hard work, a quick call to Alex confirmed that her phone would indeed register the GPS coordinates and accuracy of whichever phone she called. Exhilarated, she wondered about trying it on the Romanian troll right then and there. But worries about interfering with Wheatley's work and tipping off the villain made the idea inadvisable for the present. Instead, she allowed the exhaustion to take over, and fell asleep on the makeshift bed she had made of cushions on the floor.

*   *   *

Jakob and Felix sat in their van discussing the possibilities in detail. At length, Jakob made a call back to Maxim Kuznetsov. "There is a chance, Maxim, that we can achieve this quietly - we can put the police guard to sleep for a while with Lethepaphol which will impair his memory of the event. But it is for you to judge how her disappearance would then be interpreted. Is she in custody or under police protection? Would the police link this afternoon's failed kidnap with the Englishwoman, or would they assume she had just walked out, of her own volition, while the police guard slept? Also, there is a significant chance that our operation would be otherwise noticed or interfered with - do you want us to follow through if it means some collateral damage? An alternative is that we wait and watch - it is possible that the Englishwoman may ultimately be on her own, without the police presence, and then easily vulnerable." Jakob had respectfully summarised the options for Kuznetsov who would take responsibility for the operation, though Jakob was not convinced that Kuznetsov was sober enough to make the judgement rationally.

There were a few seconds of silence whilst Kuznetsov weighed the odds. "Go ahead," he decided at length. "A quiet abduction is preferable, of course, but the opportunity is too important to miss, even if it means stirring up the Austrian police."

Jakob put his phone back in his pocket. He looked over at Felix.

"Kuznetsov says to go ahead." Felix smiled in anticipation. Jakob laughed as he started the engine and steered the van out of the hospital car park. They lived for the opportunities to get into some action, and were still pumped up from the kidnap attempt that afternoon. Felix used his phone to arrange another hire-van for a switch early into their drive, as Jakob drove them eastward toward Klagenfurt airport.

*   *   *

Tom Wheatley had followed through on tracing the recent contacts of the Constanţa phone number that Betty had given him. The final call had turned out to be to via a cell tower in Kellerberg, just a few miles away from Villach, and that phone was still turned on. He was elated - this was a golden opportunity - that would almost certainly be the failed kidnappers. He set about requesting the more difficult task of getting a *live* trace on the phone. He hoped that if he could locate the kidnappers precisely, then he would be able to gift them to the Austrian police, and perhaps get a favour in return - the prompt homecoming of Miss Gosmore and Mr Tremaine without further questions, plus her hacked phone and the valuable photographs. Then the immediate crisis would be over and he could concentrate on working out the history of how her phone had been hacked, and the source of the security lapse. As he waited, he stood looking out of his office window in Millbank, London, down at the endless passage of traffic, along the drizzle-covered road surface reflecting the streetlights. He looked pensively across the River Thames to the MI6 headquarters building where this operation was also being monitored. Indeed, they were allowing him to use Stuart, their agent, to protect the GCHQ workers for the moment, but they would probably want to take control if there was any trouble - things might get more complicated then. He realised it was going to be a long night - he would not risk being away from his computer until this matter was settled.

Finally, the message came back with his ID tag for the live phone trace. He quickly keyed it into his computer and waited for the location to show on the screen. They had moved - the trace was no longer at Kellerberg, but a couple of miles east of Villach, and it appeared to be moving... eastward. But that meant they had driven through Villach to get onto the eastbound Autobahn. He felt a slight tension in his gut - might they have taken Betty? Her phone was still showing its location as the hospital. But he needed to make sure. He phoned Betty.

Betty was woken by the call, "Uh... Hullo?" she yawned.

"Ah, Betty, sorry, did I wake you? I just wanted to check that you are OK."

"Uh, yes. I'm fine. I'm just trying to get some sleep - it's been a long day and we've got an early start tomorrow."

"Sorry, right, no problem. I'll let you sleep then. Give me a call tomorrow morning when you get on the move. Bye."

Betty looked at the data showing on her phone screen and smiled, remembering the satisfying work she had put in earlier. She was tempted to amaze Tom Wheatley by reeling off the exact model of phone he was holding, and the coordinates of his office. That would be amusing... but incautious. Sometimes it was hard keeping secrets and resisting temptation. "Goodnight Tom."

Betty snuggled down onto the cushions again.

"Who was that on the phone?" asked George.

The question almost startled Betty - today, she had got so used to George sleeping, or just grunting an answer with a yawn. "Oh," she told him, "it was just Tom Wheatley checking that I'm... that we're OK."

George swung his feet over the side of the bed and stood up, stretching. "I'm feeling really energetic now - I was bored whilst you were asleep."

"Well it's not surprising if you get a bounce - you have been sleeping all day on that sedative medication. But sleeping is what I need to do right now - it's late and we will be leaving early tomorrow morning."

"It's not that late. Have we got anything to do in here - I feel so fidgety."

Betty sighed. George being a bit hyper was irritating when she needed the opposite.

"I know, I'll phone my wife," he declared.

"Your wife! But I thought..."

"Yes, she'll still be up - it's an hour earlier in England. Can I have the phone?"

Betty looked at George with narrowed eyes. For him to talk on the phone whilst she was trying to get to sleep seemed to be the height of insensitivity. He seemed slightly irrational as well as buzzing. But, she supposed, she needed to cut him some slack since he was the patient.

Reluctantly, she handed him the phone.

He took it and sat back on the bed. Looking at the screen he observed the almost empty contact list. "Oh... Do you know her number?" he asked.

"How the hell would I know your wife's number? retorted Betty sharply.

"Well you're a mathematician - you remember numbers."

"I don't remember numbers that I've never seen. Look, George, I think you're being a bit hyper, how's your head feeling?"

"Oh, yes, it still aches a bit. What's this strange app on the phone - I've never seen that icon before?"

"No, Geez, don't touch that George, it's dangerous, please, just don't touch that," shrilled Betty jumping up.

George looked at her, surprised. "What is it then?"

"I'll explain it to you tomorrow, OK? Trust me."

That sentence had struck a resonance, and for a couple of seconds, George seemed to recall that there was something else which Betty was going to explain tomorrow, something important. Then his mind speeded on again.

"OK, you explain it to me tomorrow." The repetition almost sounded like it came from a child, and Betty's annoyance disappeared as she felt a sudden distance between her and him, like she had never felt before.

"It's OK! I know," he declared triumphantly, "I can phone directory enquiries... Oh." He looked at her quizzically as if afraid to ask again.

"118 811." She answered the unspoken question carefully but with a tear in her eye.

Betty curled up again on the cushions, now unable to try to sleep, more because of the emotions stirred up by the strangeness of the interaction with George, than by his voice, first clumsily negotiating directory enquiries, and then wishing his wife a 'Happy New Year' and chatting aimlessly for a long time about their children and his concussion.

*   *   *

After checking on Betty, Wheatley had phoned Stuart and shared with him the ID tag for the kidnappers' phone so that Stuart could track them too. "So, Stuart, I am going to phone police command in Austria and put them on stand by. Presumably, the kidnappers will stop somewhere for the night. If you can follow them and quietly check out the building they stop at, so that we can give the police precise location instructions?"

"Yes, I can try," said Stuart, "If I set out now, I will be half an hour behind them. By the way," added Stuart, "you should contact 'EKO Cobra' rather than the local or federal police for an armed intercept here - they're the elite Police Tactical Unit, run by the interior ministry. However, assuming the kidnappers are heading East toward Romania, I am concerned that it is only three hours to the Hungarian border, so there is a good chance they may not stop in Austria tonight at all. That would complicate matters with the police forces."

"No, I don't think we can assume these guys are based in Romania," reasoned Wheatley. "They seemed to be on the scene relatively quickly after the Heiligenblut fiasco. Actually, it looks from the tracker as if they might already have stopped, in Klagenfurt, near the airport. I hope they are not going to fly out - we'll lose them if they do."

"No, there are no scheduled flights from there till morning," Stuart informed him. "Look I'll get on the road now - it'll only take me half an hour to get to Klagenfurt - I'll call you back when I get there."

Wheatley removed his gold-rimmed spectacles thoughtfully and paced the room for a minute, stretching his legs. He dearly hoped that these foreign agents were not going to get away. Wheatley was old-school. Spying was one thing, but attempting to kidnap a civilian scientist - that was outrageous. That had crossed a red line, for him. He glanced at the screen again - no movement of the kidnapper's phone tracker - still at Klagenfurt, so he sat at the desk and set about bringing his case notes up to date.

When he looked at the screen again a few minutes later, the tracker had changed position on the screen map. He looked more closely. It was moving back in the direction of Villach. But it did not seem to be following a road on the map. Were they in a field? Or was there a problem with the tracking software, he wondered? He knew that Stuart would be seeing the same thing, so he did not bother to phone him. He continued to watch the tracker dot. It also seemed to be moving faster than usual driving speed. Then, as it cut across a part of the huge Wörthersee Lake that lay between Villach and Klagenfurt, he realised that the kidnapper with the tracked phone must be in an aircraft. Damn, had Stuart been wrong about the scheduled flights, or maybe they had a private plane? But was it coincidental that it was heading in the direction of Villach? He traced a straight line on the map from Klagenfurt airport through the path of the moving target and projected it along. It crossed over the hospital in Villach. Wheatley was not given to panic, but a gnawing tightness came to his chest. A helicopter. But how the hell could they know exactly where she was? And he had sent Stuart off, driving away from Villach. Damn. No problem, he could phone Betty and tell her to abandon her room and hide somewhere else in the hospital. She could notify the police guard as well. There were still a few minutes before the helicopter would reach the hospital. He grabbed up his phone and called her - but the line was busy. Frustration compounded the tautness in his chest.

He called Stuart. "Stuart, I think they are trying to snatch her from the hospital by helicopter. Just stand by. Don't phone me - I'm trying to contact Betty now, to get her out of the room and hidden." He ended the call abruptly, and tried Betty's number again - still busy.

He texted her 'EMERGENCY, Phone Wheatley', and waited a minute for a response. The tracker was already showing a location perilously close to the hospital.

*   *   *

George had finally run out of things to say and, somewhat reluctantly, ended the call with his wife. He looked idly at the screen wondering if there was someone else he could phone, but then noticed there was a text notification and clicked to read it. "Oh Betty, there's a text message here from Tom Wheatley - it says 'EMERGENCY - phone Tom Wheatley'."

"What!" Betty almost sprang from her makeshift bed and grabbed the phone from George. At that moment it rang.

"Betty, are you there?"

"Yes - it's me, Tom."

"Listen, the kidnappers are landing a helicopter on the hospital roof helipad. Get the hell out of that room, onto another floor and hide. They'll be there any second."

Betty drew in a very deep breath. Priorities immediately came into focus. She first started the 'killer app' she had written for her phone and keyed one or two settings - it was her only weapon. Then she hesitated a second - should she try to get George out too, in his rather slow-witted state? Or would he be safe as he was not the target? Or would she feel guilty if she left him? But she never had the chance to finalise a decision - it was too late. She heard a muffled fracas outside and then the door burst open, and a burly man in black bounded confidently into the room, gun in hand, instantaneously scanning round to assess who was in the room. That was Betty's chance. For a frozen instant, he looked from George to Betty and to George again, presumably judging him the greater threat. The would-be kidnapper was 4 metres in front of her. All Betty needed to do was press the button. But now that she was faced with the reality, she felt she could not do it - kill a man in cold blood.

Surprisingly, in that instant, it was George, belying his confused state, who acted first. He lunged at the man. But he was no match for a trained assassin. The man swung an arm hard as George connected, knocking him down, and then fired his gun, shooting George through the head. The sound of the shot was surprisingly muffled, but the effect was brutal. George's head jerked at an uncanny angle and blood spattered the floor. The effect on Betty however, was galvanising. Previously unable to act, she now made a small movement with her feet, judging the distance, and pressed the button. Satisfied that he had dispensed with George, the man turned toward Betty again, just as the lethal zap cracked loudly, the circular flash appearing to cut across his head and chest. He folded and fell with a stifled agonised cry, briefly writhing on the floor, close to the stilled body of George. Betty thrust the phone into her leggings, grabbing her coat around her, intending to get away. She knew that the phone would not be a weapon again until the i-vector equipment had re-charged - around 50 minutes. She felt nothing yet, but looked back at the scene on the floor. It would have become a horrific scene etched in her memory, had that memory been allowed to form.

Jakob and Felix had simply overpowered Lukas before he had had time to react, and now Jakob had been carefully arranging Lukas's limp, lightly-drugged body in the chair to make it look as if he had just fallen asleep. Jakob, though he would have much preferred a 'quiet' abduction, was not particularly alarmed by the sound of Felix's silenced gun firing, but was taken aback by the unrecognisable loud cracking sound that followed. He quickly finished arranging Lukas and dashed into the room with his gun drawn to find his intended victim, Betty, looking down at the bodies of Felix and some other man. Without

91

waiting to work out what had happened, he dived onto Betty pinning her to the ground, pulled out another syringe of the tranquilliser drug from his pocket and, stabbing the needle into her neck, he emptied the contents into her bloodstream. During the couple of seconds it took for her to lose consciousness, he took stock of the situation. The cracking sound, which presumably heralded Felix's misfortune, may have alerted unwanted attention - he had very little time. Curious, he checked Felix's pulse - Felix was dead - there was a burn across his face. Jakob picked up the limp body of Betty and carried her quickly out of the room, along the corridor, to the lift, up one floor and out into the cold night air of the roof. The helicopter's rotors were still turning - he had told the pilot to keep the engine running for a 'hot load'. But the turning rotors were causing a strong blast of cold air, against which he struggled as he approached the helicopter. A couple of times it made him slip on the light layer of snow covering the roof, and he realised why the pilot had argued that a 'hot load' was dangerous. He would remember next time, but still, it would save them a valuable minute or two. He laid Betty out gently across the rear seats of the helicopter, not because he cared for her comfort, but because he wanted to maintain the illusion to the pilot that they were airlifting a medical emergency over to a clinic in Klagenfurt. This was the story they had told to him, and which he had apparently accepted, along with a small wad of money to depress his curiosity. The pilot had quailed slightly on finding that the landing lights had not been illuminated at the hospital helipad, but after sharp words from Jakob, he had been cowed into landing the helicopter without fuss, as it was a 'medical necessity'.

Jakob jumped into one of the remaining seats, slammed the door shut and urged the pilot to "Go. Go quickly," lying, in explanation, that his colleague was staying behind to complete the paperwork. The aircraft lifted away, and Jakob allowed himself a deep breath as the immediate adrenaline rush wore off, and he contemplated the state of affairs. The abduction scene was a mess - it had been anything but quiet. Felix was out of the picture. Jakob might allow himself to feel some regret later, but for now, it simply meant he had to complete the operation himself, and speed would be essential initially, since it was only a matter of time before the police were alerted, and instigating a hunt. The few minutes flying time back to Klagenfurt airfield would seem like an eternity. But their van was ready at the airfield, and Felix had pre-arranged a van switch after less than an hour's drive that would also put him across the border into Slovenia, away from the Austrian police. He had loaded the woman with more drug than normal because he had realised that he would be working on his own - she should be out for several hours he reckoned.

*   *   *

As the aircraft skirted the Wörthersee Lake, Stuart, with consternation, was watching both the kidnapper's phone tracker and Betty's phone tracker, now proceeding together as one dot on his phone screen. Stranded halfway between Villach and Klagenfurt on the lake road, he could actually see the helicopter making a beeline back towards Klagenfurt. Despairing for Betty's safety, but encouraged that he had a good 'fix' on them, he set off driving back in the direction of Klagenfurt - at least they would not have too much of a start on him, he reckoned.

*   *   *

Jakob was not expecting trouble at Klagenfurt airfield, it was still only minutes after the abduction. It would be too soon for the police to have pieced together what had happened, and to have alerted any patrol nearby. Nevertheless, he was relieved when they arrived to find the airfield relatively deserted and quiet. He thanked the helicopter pilot for his efforts and said he would now hurry the patient to the clinic in Klagenfurt town, carrying her from the helicopter out to his van parked next to the helicopter servicing area. Finally out of sight of the pilot, he laid her on a rough bed of blankets in the back of the van, and quickly put ties around her hands and legs as a precaution, though he did not expect her to become conscious for some hours. He hurriedly checked her pockets for a phone that might just enable her to be tracked, but found none, since Betty had concealed hers down her leggings. Then with some sense of relief, he drove out of the airport entrance and onto the autobahn circling the town, soon turning off on a minor road southwards towards the Slovenian border.

*   *   *

"I don't have any detail from the Villach police yet," Tom Wheatley was updating Stuart as the latter drove in pursuit of the electronic trackers. "The police are arriving to investigate the scene at the hospital room now. All I've said to them is that we think we have a lead on the kidnappers and we'll let them know if we get a location or vehicle registration."

    "Yes, let's keep it to ourselves because, at the present rate, I

93

won't catch them up before they have crossed the border from Austria into Slovenia," reasoned Stuart. "So any armed response unit would have to be activated out of the Slovenian capital, Ljubljana, anyway, but we still don't know which way they are ultimately headed. Best to keep our options open - if we tell the police too much it may hinder myself taking any direct action."

"OK then. By the way, Schweiger is very apologetic - he has promised to expedite getting Betty's phone and those photos to us straight away, so at least that is one problem solved. Actually, I feel rather sorry for him - he has been made to look incompetent - but I don't think he could reasonably have been expected to have used greater protection for Betty. Ah, that's him calling back on the other line - I'll get back to you with more details after I've spoken to him."

"Guten Abend Herr Wheatley. Ja, I have arrived at the hospital now. I'm afraid I have bad news for you - your man, Herr Tremaine is dead - he was shot, apparently during the abduction."

Wheatley sighed. "Oh no... these people are behaving outrageously. So what else have you been able to determine?"

"Essentially, Miss Gosmore is gone and one other man is dead - we assume he was one of those attempting the abduction - he had a gun and drugs on him. My police officer who was on guard outside the room, appeared to be asleep. But we had trouble arousing him - I suspect he was drugged - he has no recollection of the event at all. So, we are doing a blood test on him. Then we will do a gunshot residue test on the dead man, and seek to match his gun with the bullet in Mr Tremaine - that should tie up that murder. But the dead man has no bullet wound on first inspection, though he has a burn across his face. I have not talked with you yet about this, Herr Wheatley, but the two would-be kidnappers from Heiligenblut were also afflicted with burns, indeed possibly they were killed by burns before crashing, which makes it look very much as if Miss Gosmore is defending herself with some sort of unorthodox weapon. I confess though, we have found no hint of any such weapon in her luggage or on her person, and the burn injuries are like nothing we have ever seen before. I am hoping you can help me out on this Herr Wheatley, as it will be very difficult to close these two cases with the evidence as it is. I realise of course, that Miss Gosmore would have been certainly acting in self-defence."

"Yes," acknowledged Wheatley noncommittally, "Miss Gosmore

phoned me earlier and told me that you had some strange autopsy results that you were struggling to interpret, but she was adamant that she had nothing to do with their deaths. I suggest that you send me copies of the autopsy results and we will study them and see if we can make some sense of them."

"Thank you, Herr Wheatley, I will do that, thank you. Now, I have officers over at Klagenfurt airport - they have located the helicopter pilot already. Apparently, he said he had no idea that the flight was an abduction - he was told it was an urgent medical transfer to a clinic in Klagenfurt. He confirmed that he flew two men to Villach Hospital, but only one flew back with an unconscious female patient - so I would assume she, Miss Gosmore, has been drugged also - I will let you know the details when we have analysed the syringe from the dead man's pocket. Unfortunately, the pilot could give us no information about the vehicle in which they left the airport, but we may be able to identify that from the airport CCTV - I will let you know. Again, I am so sorry that this has happened - I have no idea how they found Miss Gosmore - we kept her location secret, but I admit I was not expecting these abductors to be so persistent and audacious. Villach, here, is a quiet city - we do not normally have to deal with such brazen and violent crime."

Wheatley checked the progress of the trackers on the kidnapper's car and Stuart's car on his computer screen, and spent some minutes trying to anticipate the route, and the mental reasoning of the kidnapper. He researched the sequence of events that he anticipated were most likely to happen, and then phoned Stuart again to brief him.

"OK Stuart, so this is how I see it now. Firstly, Schweiger has told me, from the pilot's account, that whilst there were two men in the helicopter going to Villach hospital, only one returned, with an unconscious Betty in the helicopter, to Klagenfurt. And indeed, we know that one of the kidnappers was killed at the hospital. So most likely, there is only one kidnapper in the vehicle you are pursuing, which will make it somewhat easier for you during any intercept. There were syringes of drug found on the dead kidnapper at the hospital, so it seems likely that Betty has been tranquillised - probably Lethepaphol - that seems to be their tranquilliser of choice these days.

"The kidnapper's van seems," he continued, "to be heading for Ljubljana. From there he has a choice of routes - either through Hungary or Croatia. Either way, the frequent crossing of borders makes it difficult to arrange for police intercepts in good time. But I assume he will be aiming to do a vehicle switch as soon as possible to confound any observations of the original vehicle, and the only logical place to do that on this route, at this time of night, would be Ljubljana airport. I have done calculations of your and their average speeds, and the difference suggests to me that you will be able to catch up to them fairly comfortably by then. Ljubljana is a small airport - there are just a handful of departures and arrivals between now and midnight, so there will be people around, but not crowds. The vehicle hire businesses are sited at the entrance to the main terminal, which is just a couple of minutes walk away from the main car park. There are a few bays outside those hire businesses, but I would not expect him to park there and transfer Betty between vehicles - those bays are right by the entrances and it might well attract attention. So, I would expect him to park in the main car park, walk over to the terminal to hire the new vehicle, and then drive that back into the car park to transfer Betty, which should give you a few minutes to access his old vehicle with Betty inside. Oh, and you take a ticket for parking on the way in - first 15 minutes is free, so if you're quick you can just drive out the exit using that ticket. Otherwise, you'll have to go over to the terminal first to pay at the parking automat."

"OK," acknowledged Stuart, "and what's the environment of the car park like - much cover?"

"Hang on." Wheatley switched the google maps view to street view. "Mmm... it's flat and open, I'm afraid. No trees or cover. Some high overhead lighting."

"And what about the vehicle - do we know what type yet? Have you got a break-in protocol for me?"

"Sorry Stuart, the Austrian police talked about checking CCTV, but haven't got back to me yet - it's only been half an hour. Perhaps if you catch-up to the kidnapper enough to observe the vehicle type, and tell me? Then I can give you a protocol. You're about a kilometre behind them at the moment, with about 10 kilometres to the airport"

"No, I'd rather hang back until the airport approach road - the last thing I want to do is spook him. Anyway, I've got precious little in the way of tools with me," mused Stuart pensively.

"OK, if you want any other information just ring me," concluded Wheatley.

Wheatley sat back and watched the markers on his screen getting closer to the airport and converging - he could do nothing more to help now.

*   *   *

Stuart used a little more throttle as he got closer to the airport. He could see two vehicles on the road ahead. The nearest, about 200 metres in front, he could now see was a car, and another 300 metres in front of that was what he thought would be the target. As it turned on a roundabout to the right, the change in direction of the tracker on his screen confirmed his theory. He could now see that it was a van. Stuart turned his phone to silent, and put it in his pocket. Stuart and the car in front also followed the same route heading into the airport. Then he could see that they were skirting the car park to his right, and after another right turn, they were approaching the car park entrance, which the van was already going through. The car in front was keeping him further back than he would have wanted, but he watched very carefully the route of the van as it proceeded toward the far end of the car park which was sparsely populated with cars - presumably, the kidnapper expected less attention at that end. The car in front headed straight up and found a vacant space near the middle. Stuart took one of the side lanes driving slowly. He saw the van driver get out and start walking swiftly back toward the entrance.

The clock was now ticking. Stuart noted the kidnapper's appearance. A woman stepped out of the car that had been in front, pulled a bag out, and also started back toward the entrance. Stuart parked his car about three-quarters of the way up and opened the boot as if he were attending to luggage. Behind the boot, he was able to observe the van driver without being visible. The van driver looked back to the van once, but did not seem overly jumpy. Stuart's military experience in Special Operations was now kicking in. He noted the positions of larger vehicles around which might provide cover, and checked out the positions of the overhead lights, and where they might throw shadows of him. He could not see any CCTV cameras anywhere near.

The van driver was well out of sight now, so Stuart closed the boot of his car, and marched confidently over to the van, keeping a hand on the gun in his pocket - he didn't think there was another kidnapper in the van, but nothing was certain yet. As he got close, he saw there was indeed no one in the front seats. He reached the van and listened - nothing. Gun in hand, he tried the side door handle - locked. He tapped the side door. "Betty, hey Betty, can you hear me, it's Stuart - can you open the door?" No reply.

Stuart took a foldable lock pick tool from his pocket. He bent down and quickly let the air out of the rear tyre with the end of a pick. Fortunately, the kidnapper had parked the van with the side door facing away from the entrance, so Stuart was able to work on the lock whilst keeping watch through the cab side windows toward the entrance for any reappearance of the kidnapper with his newly hired van. Stuart inserted his tension wrench into the lock and applied a little turning pressure. With the other hand, he inserted the pick rake, and started scrubbing the pick gently back and forth. Once or twice, he thought he had most of the driver pins caught on the plug, but at least one of the pins was resisting. It seemed like he would have to pick each pin individually, but would there be time? Reluctantly he withdrew the rake and tried a single-ridge pick. Some progress, but it was taking far too long. A vehicle was entering. Stuart put away the tool in his pocket, and braced himself for action. No, it was only a car. But would it park in a position where the driver would be able to see what he was doing? Stuart waited as it drew closer. Finally, it turned in to a spot, short of his position. He waited whilst the driver got out, pulled a case out of the back and strode off back toward the entrance, oblivious to Stuart's presence. Stuart reluctantly started the picking procedure over again. Progress - he felt the plug tantalisingly close to turning.

Another vehicle was coming through the entrance. It was a van - almost certainly the kidnapper. Too late now for the lock. Stuart slipped the kit back in his pocket and watched through the side window of the cab. He did not yet know whether the driver would park next to the van on this side, or perhaps back-to-back. The new van was coming round his side - he quickly ducked around the back of the stationary van to avoid being seen, and then round the far side. He would have to be careful not to make changes in shadow that would be noticed. Stuart dropped down low so he could see the driver's feet by looking underneath the van. The engine of the new van was left running - good, he did not have to worry about moving so quietly. He would have to be quick though - anyone entering the car park would have headlights pointing straight at him where he was. He saw two feet as the driver jumped down from the van. The sound of a side door being slid open. Wait for the other door. Was that a vehicle at the entrance? Now, the sound of the other door sliding open. Stuart moved fast like a cat around the back of the van, and into the gap between the two vans. The kidnapper had his head inside the original van as Stuart had envisaged, and so was late seeing Stuart coming. Stuart dived at his head, banging it onto the van floor and getting his fingers hard onto the carotid artery pressure points of the unfortunate kidnapper. But this man was no pushover. He rammed his elbow backwards into Stuart's ribs. Stuart winced but held on, committed to his move. The kidnapper's hand went into his pocket pulling out a gun. Stuart rammed his knee hard against the kidnapper's arm to prevent him aiming the gun backwards, and in just a few seconds the kidnapper succumbed to the attack on his pressure points, slumping forward onto the van floor, unconscious. Now, time was of the essence. Stuart took the man's gun and slipped it into his own pocket. For the first time, he looked properly inside the van he had been trying to break into. Betty was lying there, unconscious, on the van floor, hands and legs tied.

Stuart had no time for sympathetic emotion. He scooped Betty up and placed her gently onto the floor of the new van, slamming the side door shut. He jumped into the new van, which still had its engine running, and drove off toward the entrance. But then he remembered Wheatley's detailed briefing on the car park system. His ticket would let him out of the exit if he had been no longer than 15 minutes. How long had that all taken? - he had no idea - time froze during the stress and adrenaline of active operation. If the ticket would not open the exit barrier, then he had a choice. He could either crash through it - which would no doubt get the attention of a CCTV camera there, or he could walk over to the terminal entrance to pay for parking time on the automat - but that would mean leaving Betty unattended, and the kidnapper would be regaining consciousness by now. Both bad choices. He reached the barrier, leaned out the side window, pushed his ticket into the slot and hoped. A whirring inside the ticket machine. The barrier was still down. Stuart braced himself to reverse and accelerate at the barrier. But then the barrier calmly opened. With enormous relief, Stuart accelerated out of the car park exit onto the road. Looking back, he thought he could see a figure, doubled over, leaning with both hands, on the old van.

Stuart drove for a couple of kilometres back in the direction he had come before pulling off the road briefly, knowing the kidnapper would anyway be unable to pursue with a flat tyre. He opened the side door and jumped in. He pulled a pen knife out of his pocket and cut the ties from Betty's hands and feet, noting that one wrist was red and chafed. He tried to rouse her, but she was still deeply unconscious. He checked her pulse and was somewhat reassured. He removed his overcoat, and emptying the pockets of hard items - knife, tools, guns and phone, he made a bed of the overcoat, laying her gently on it. Then he closed the side door again and drove on, soon taking the turning marked Trieste. He had already decided to drive west, quickly crossing the border out of Slovenia, avoiding Austria and Eastern Europe - it would be a long drive, skirting the Alps, and then North through Switzerland, toward the UK. He knew he could not stop in a hotel, with Betty unconscious, so resigned himself to getting as much mileage as possible done during that night.

*   *   *

Wheatley had, meanwhile, been glued to a skeleton of the action by watching the three phone trackers - kidnapper, Betty and Stuart on his computer screen. He had seen Stuart's signal converge on the other two as he approached the car park. Then Stuart had turned his phone off so as not to be disturbed during the action. Wheatley had expected this, but then he had to endure a quarter hour of tension, having no idea what was actually happening, before he finally saw the signals from the phones of the kidnapper and Betty separate, and then Stuart's phone finally on again showing the same location as Betty. At that point, he had allowed himself a small celebratory drink - it had been a tense and worrying few hours.

Once settled on the main road to Trieste, Stuart called Wheatley to brief him. "Hi Tom, yes, I have Betty safely in the back of a van - she's still unconscious, but seems OK apart from chafed wrists where they tied her."

"That's great news, Stuart, I can't commend you enough."

Stuart took a deep breath. "Yes. Action is never easy," he replied wistfully. Now that the adrenaline was wearing off, he could reflect on the fine line between success and failure, and the suppressed fear.

"I know. I understand," Wheatley replied with genuine sympathy. "So, details: Did you leave behind anything that would interest the police?"

"No, I didn't use a gun. I left the kidnapper with a couple of bruises and a flat tire, so that should be the end of it. I'm driving the van that the kidnapper newly hired at Ljubljana airport. I will change it for a car as soon as Betty wakes, but until then, I'll get some distance and borders between us and Slovenia."

"Excellent, Stuart. Keep me posted on any developments - I'm going home to sleep easy myself now, thanks to your good work," laughed Wheatley.

Shortly before midnight, Stuart drove across the unchecked border into Italy.

Chapter 6
Back to Basics

The journey was long but uneventful. Stuart stopped twice during the night to refuel the van, and checked each time on Betty. She still seemed very deeply asleep. After 6 hours of monotonous driving on the tedious Italian motorway, he was relieved to finally turn off and head north into Switzerland. The roads were more difficult now, with frequent turns as they weaved around the changes in altitude, but they at least provided some interest and demanded attention from a tired driver. It was still dark.

Another two hours on into Switzerland, and Stuart found the road ahead closed. With reluctance and now feeling very tired after 9 or 10 hours of driving, he took the sign-posted diversion. Finally, after another half hour Stuart decided that he really needed coffee and food, and more importantly a toilet, so he decided that at the next opportunity, he would do a pit stop.

*   *   *

Now, after several hours of empty, blank unconsciousness, Betty's torpor was beginning to lift, but only to the level of strange disconnected dreams.

She was sitting in the middle of a four-poster bed. A man stood at each corner. She had a different secret from each of the men, and none could communicate with each other... She faced each in turn. To the first, she said, 'I know where you are,' but he could not hear. To the second, she said, 'I will tell you tomorrow,' and he went away. To the third, she said, 'I did not do it.' And he replied, 'I do not believe you.' To the fourth, she said, 'Please do not ask me,' but he still looked quizzically at her...

Now she was running around barefoot in a field. She wanted to stop but people kept running toward her so she had to run away again. One man said he would let her out of the field if she would answer his question, but she knew that if she answered his question then he would run after her too... She knew that she could knock these people over by hitting them with her phone but she couldn't let the others see her do it...

Now she was walking down a road and the end was in sight, but the others would not let her get to the end, and she did not want to reach the end with the others harassing her, she wanted to walk to the end in peace...

Then looking back she saw there were several versions of her - some were running in the field, some were walking down the road being harassed, some were flying and being chased, one was writhing in agony - all were doing something different, but none was at peace... All she wanted was peace. In the dream, she covered her eyes and squatted down. But there was no peace - she could still hear the mayhem around her... So, she tried covering her ears... Still, there was noise... One ear was hurting... Then deep sleep again...

Still, the people were barging into her, always barging into her from the back... And there was something pressing her face... And a monotonous rumble... always there... interspersed with random bumps to her back... and to her ear... She tried to move her ear away from the bumps... Yes, that was much more comfortable... Deep sleep again...

She was flying free... Then a jerking movement... And another... And each time she jerked, she lost height... Until eventually, she was lying on the ground... And now the jerks were coming from the ground... And that monotonous rumble still... Then finally the question began to be asked, in a very disconnected way... What was making those bumping movements to her back? Where am I, to be hearing that monotonous rumble? Ah, It's like I am lying on the floor in a moving vehicle... She felt some satisfaction in working out that conclusion, and drifted off to sleep again...

She slowly came to again, and eventually revisited the idea that she was lying in a moving vehicle... But why am I lying in a vehicle?... What happened before this to cause me to be here?... Then the word 'kidnap' came back to her... They were trying to kidnap me... But they failed - their van crashed at Heiligenblut... So why am I here now?... Is this another timeline?... She tried hard to think back to what had happened before this... But it was difficult to put together a chain of events... She remembered the police station... She remembered skiing... And the little church with the piano... And a big grand piano... Where was that?... Ah, a hotel with a warm swimming pool... and George... and then she remembered the crashed van near Heiligenblut and shivered at the memory... And a hospital room... And driving in a blizzard... None of it seemed to fit together... Then she briefly lapsed back into sleep again...

When she came to next time, she found the beginnings of motivation... So, if she had been kidnapped, then she needed to try to get away... She tried moving her head, her arms and legs... They all seemed to work, if a little sluggishly... She felt over the rest of her body... She was lying on a thick woollen coat that was partially cushioning her from the bumps of the van riding the road... and there was something very familiar about the coat, but she couldn't remember what, something good about it... Suddenly her hands found the phone concealed in her leggings... Ah yes, the weapon... She pulled it out and looked at it... she seemed to remember that she had designed how to make it work, but that seemed like a different world, very complicated, almost like she was another person then... But it didn't matter... She could remember that she just had to point it and press the button when the green light showed it was ready... Yes, the green indicator was on... So, if she pointed it at the driver of the van... she looked around... the glow from the phone screen showed her where the bulkhead was... the driver would be just a half metre in front of that... She remembered she had to get the distance right... She tried to sit up... yes, she could manage that, though it was an effort... She lost balance as the van bumped, reminding her of the speed on the road... No, she shouldn't do it whilst the van was moving, the van would crash... and she would get hurt... she didn't even have a seat belt on... No, she would wait until the van stopped, at a junction, or a traffic light - it didn't matter, then use the weapon... then she would get out and run... She looked at the side and rear door handles... no problem, she could do that... she would lie down again and wait for the van to stop... she snuggled down against the warm coat and immediately drifted off to sleep again...

A while later she jolted awake... the van was not moving, it had stopped... a little adrenalin helped to clear her mind and she sat upright... It had to be now... she pointed the phone judging the distance to just beyond the bulkhead and pressed the button... There was a sharp cracking sound... it had worked... she noticed that the phone was almost out of battery so she switched it off... With some elation, she grabbed the back door handle and swung open the rear door... a blast of very cold air... She reached back in, grabbed the overcoat that she had been lying on, pulled it around her and walked unsteadily away from the van without looking back... There was a bus of some sort, pointed in the opposite direction, not far across the road... She trudged through the snow, still physically shaky, but steadfastly focussed on getting to the bus... there was a woman paying the bus-driver... Betty climbed the step onto the bus, felt in her pocket for some cash... She handed a note to the driver, who seemed to be asking her a question in German that Betty could not understand... probably asking the destination, she thought... 'Ja, Ja,' she muttered and handed over another note which looked like it was certainly large enough for any destination, then she walked on down the aisle of the bus to find a seat, ignoring any further interaction with the driver... She slumped down in the seat, and, exhausted by the effort of the short walk, fell asleep again almost instantly... The driver shrugged, pocketed the notes and drove on.

When Betty next came to, there were very few people left on the bus. She stretched to loosen up the cricks that had come from sleeping in a slouched sitting position. Indeed, awareness of her body was now demanding more of her attention - she felt very hungry and desperately needed a pee. She looked out of the window - dawn was now beginning to illuminate a vista of mountains, forest and snow, with just the occasional building. Up to now, she had not even considered where she was going - she had focussed entirely on getting away from the kidnap van. She decided that finding somewhere to pee was the most urgent issue, so she pressed the stop request button. She had assumed that the driver would continue to the next official stop, but he pulled over almost straight away, and she worked her way up the aisle to the door, casually thanked the driver and stepped off. She hoped he would forget her, and where he had dropped her, if anyone came asking.

As the bus trundled away, she found herself in the middle of nowhere, and there was a cold breeze blowing. She pulled the overcoat tighter round her... Probably best to get off this bus route... There was a small lane a short distance on the left. She trudged over there and started down it. There was no traffic on it, though there were tread marks in the snow from a vehicle or two. No buildings in sight. She felt confident enough to stop and relieve herself here, but she was still unsteady and as she squatted, she fell back sitting her bum onto the cold snow. At first she cursed, but then laughed out loud at the humour in the ridiculous situation. That task over, she pulled the overcoat around her again and was about to set off when a recollection hit her. The puddle she had made in the snow reminded her of something... Ah, yes, she had wrung out some wet clothes into the snow recently... Why?... She started walking on down the lane with more vigour, trying to recall the context of wringing out wet clothes in the snow... But the sequence of events would not come to her... The lane was winding on and on - no sign of any buildings... Perhaps she should have ridden the bus to its terminus - at least there would be some civilisation there... But no, she felt she would be safer hidden away somewhere remote until she could at least work out what had happened... She walked on for what seemed like ages...

106

The lane twisted and turned, always promising something around the next bend, but only delivering more mountain views, forest and snow. After a long time, with still no buildings in sight, she began to wonder if she should turn and go back to the road with the bus route. But she could feel fatigue coming on again, and it was so far back. She decided she was past the point of no return and continued fatalistically. A dog barked in the distance. She preferred to believe it was a welcome sign of habitation rather than a threat. She walked on. Still no sign of a building. She was getting very weak again now - that overwhelming feeling of needing to sleep was creeping back. She knew she could not walk much further, but she also knew she must. As she staggered on, the blinding white of the snow, all around, was conspiring with her faintness to compromise her ability to see, but she lurched unsteadily on, with her vision tunnelling, just managing to keep to the lane...

The dog was barking again, much closer this time. She was very cold. She realised she had been lying in the snow, having passed out... She didn't know how long she had been there... Then an old lady, with long grey hair tied in a bun, and bundled up against the snow, was looking down at her. She was carrying an axe. But it was something about the hair-bun that first grabbed Betty's attention - she half-remembered doing her hair that way... recently?

"Oh mein armes Kind, was ist passiert?" (Oh my poor child, what has happened?)

"Uh, I'm lost. I'm very lost," sobbed Betty pitifully, as her rationality finally began to kick in enough to alarm even herself about her situation.

"Komm, come with me, we need to get you in the warm... Get away Otto," she reprimanded the dog who was licking Betty's face. She bent down and helped Betty stand, then pulled Betty's arm around her neck. Betty was both unsteady, and stiff with cold. Thankfully, the old woman seemed surprisingly strong as she supported Betty in walking on a little further down the lane. Again, Betty felt reminded of something she couldn't quite recall, of another recent time when someone had their arm round her. Shortly, a break in the forest of firs revealed a small, simple but picturesque chalet, with wisps of smoke issuing from a chimney. Betty's eyes filled with tears of relief at the sight.

The old woman led her straight over to the fireplace and took the overcoat from her. Betty knelt down in front of the fire, soaking in the relaxing and restorative warmth, but then, overcome with exhaustion, she lay down, curled up and fell asleep again.

She dreamed that George had talked of killing the dog, and then un-killing it again, so the dog did not find her and she died, or the dog did find her, and she lived. But this was the first time since being at the hospital that she had been asleep in a warm and quiet environment, so ultimately she relaxed completely and slept deeply without dreaming for a time.

*   *   *

When Betty finally opened her eyes to the friendly warm flickering of flame in the hearth, she felt much more composed. She watched the flames darting around and soaked up the life-giving glow for a minute. The old woman had put a pillow under Betty's head whilst she was sleeping, and was now watching over her from a chair next to the fire whilst she sewed. Betty sat up languidly and the two met in a smile, silent for a moment.

Betty spoke first. "Thank you. Thank you for all your kindness."

"Kindness costs nothing," responded the old woman. "How are you feeling now my dear? I checked your brow for a fever, but you had none, though if you want I can go and fetch a doctor?"

"No, I am not ill… Well I *am* ill, but that is not the problem," added Betty wistfully.

"Ah… Well, my name is Greta. And, if you would like to tell me the story of how you came to me, I am more than happy to listen." She cocked her head in anticipation, but continued sewing.

Betty took a deep breath. "Thank you, Greta. I'm not exactly sure myself, what has happened to me - I seem to be having trouble remembering - there is a disconnect - something has happened to my mind, I think - I seem to be sleeping a lot and feel very weak. But the reason that I ended up here is that I was kidnapped and then escaped." Greta suddenly stopped sewing and looked at Betty with concern. "At least I think I was kidnapped, I can't actually remember it happening. I remember waking up in the back of a van. When the van stopped, I used…" Betty paused for a moment. "I used a weapon on the driver, then I fled, well, walked actually, because I was so weak. I saw a bus and just got on it, to put some distance between me, and the van. I think I must have slept for quite a long time on the bus. When I finally got off I

108

had no idea where I was, so I just started walking down a lane, away from the road and the traffic. In a sense, I wanted to get away from civilisation and get lost, because that seemed the safest that I could be from the kidnapper. But I came a long way without finding any people, any houses, and I started to get very weak again. I think I must have collapsed because I woke up on the ground where you found me."

"Well, actually it was Otto that found you. He is a Bernese mountain dog - they are very finely attuned to searching for people - he came back barking at me to come out, so I knew that something was wrong." Betty looked over at the dog who was sitting a little way away, and wondered if she was stealing his usual place in front of the fire, but he looked content enough.

"Thank you, Otto," she whispered, and he padded over to her for some petting.

"So I don't quite follow why you think you had been kidnapped, just because you were in the back of a van?" asked Greta.

"Ah. Well, it's because they had already tried, but failed, a day or so ago... in fact... yes, I think they tried a second time. I can just recall the police Inspector telling us at the hospital - the kidnappers thought I was still in the car we had hired, and so they ended up abducting some poor innocent lady, but only briefly, thank goodness."

"Ah, so do you want to let the police know what has happened?" asked Greta. "I'm afraid there is no phone reception here, but I can walk into the village and phone from there if you would like?"

"Thank you, Greta, but definitely not. The police were supposed to be protecting me but... Well, all I really want is to get home, once I have cleared my head. So you mentioned a village - where are we exactly?"

"You are in the Sertig valley, my dear - near the village of Dörfli."

Betty shook her head. "Sorry, I've never heard of that - where is the nearest big town?"

"Well, Davos is on the other side of the mountain behind us - have you heard of that?"

"Oh, yes. So we are in Switzerland - I hadn't realised. That's strange - I would have expected the kidnappers to drive east," reasoned Betty aloud.

Greta put down her sewing. "Well, since I don't need to go for the doctor or police, I would like to make us a late breakfast," she said rising from her chair. "Would you like to help me find some eggs?"

She watched as Betty tried to stand, ready to step in to support her, if need be. "Thank you, Greta, I'm feeling stronger now." Greta picked up the axe from beside her chair and headed for the door with Betty following.

"I was about to chop some logs for the fire when Otto raised the alarm, but I can do that later," she explained. Betty accompanied her into a large paddock area. There were goats at the far end and some hens pecking around near the door. Greta led Betty over to the hen houses, gave her a basket, and showed her where to look for the freshly laid eggs, whilst she, herself, went to milk the goats. Betty was enchanted. She very carefully felt for eggs amongst the bedding, and placed each of them gently in the basket. One of the hens made a fuss, squawking and flapping its wings as she disturbed it, but she persevered. She felt like a proud child carrying the basket of finds over to Greta. But the goat that was being milked fidgeted and tried to back off as she approached.

"Whoa, still now," Greta soothed the goat. "Don't come too close too quickly, child. The animals get nervous very easily when they see things they are unaccustomed to."

"Oh, sorry." Betty apologised, her proud child now feeling rather ignorant and silly.

"So, take the eggs into the kitchen, and then grab that big shovel by the wall. Scrape the snow off some of the grass so the hens can peck at the ground."

Betty did as she was bade, a smile coming to her face as she enjoyed the feeling of being useful in such basic ways.

Greta was back from the goats with two jugs of warm milk, incongruously steaming slightly in the cold air. "Right that's good, that's enough. You need to leave the hens some work to do - it's healthy for them to have a purpose. Work is important for humans too," she added philosophically. Now, that bin over there - two big handfuls of grain - scatter it about for the hens to find, and mind you put the lid back on tight, or they'll be getting in there." Greta retreated into the chalet with the milk.

Betty went over to the bin and lifted the lid. Instantly, the hens were madly running in her direction, excited. She scattered the grain and watched in fascination as the hens obsessively descended on the pockets of feed, busily searching out every grain. She watched them for a minute and then looked around. The valley was deeply formed - imposing, heavily wooded mountains rising on each side, but the sun was now just visible looking farther on, down the valley. She went back into the chalet kitchen to find Greta cutting slices of bread, and watching over a large battered frying pan on a wood-burning stove, sizzling with frying eggs.

Greta looked up and smiled at her. "OK, my dear?"

"Yes, this place is delightful, Greta. You live here alone?"

"Yes dear, alone since my husband died ten years ago. But I have Otto for company." The dog was lying dutifully in the corner of the kitchen, paying attention to the conversation.

"So how far is the village - do you go there very often?"

"It's about 4 kilometres down the valley. In the summer months, when there is no snow, I walk there about once a week for supplies, but not so much in the winter. I have lived in this chalet all my life. I was born and brought up in the old ways, when we grew our own food and made our own clothes - and I still do that as much as possible. But I am not proud - I will buy jam from the village if I run out... and coffee beans." She laughed as she ground some beans, and doused them with hot water from a copper kettle that had been sitting on the stove. "We brought up a couple of children here. But they were clever and wanted to move to the city when they were grown up. They come and visit sometimes, and bring my grandchildren to see me. My son insisted that I had electricity installed here - he worries about me coping on my own. But I don't use it much - I prefer the light of a candle - It's softer and calmer." She handed Betty a large plate of breakfast, and followed it with a cup of coffee onto which she gently poured a little cream off the top of the fresh milk.

"There, eat up, my child, this will help get your strength back."

"Thank you so much, Greta."

They ate in silence for a minute. Betty was absorbed by how good the home produce tasted. "And you made the bread yourself?" she asked.

Greta nodded. "And the butter."

"It's all absolutely delicious." Then her mind was trying to recall something - another recent meal that was especially delicious. But the memory would not come. This feeling - similar to 'déjà vu', though unrequited, was happening frequently, and was so frustrating.

111

After the meal, Betty helped Greta with the washing-up.

"Thank you, my dear. Now I need to chop some wood for the fire. We are running low - that is the task I was about to do when Otto found you. Would you like to help me or would you prefer to rest?"

"Oh, no, I would love to help." Betty was relishing all these basic living tasks, and it was also satisfying for her to feel that she was contributing, rather than imposing on Greta's hospitality.

Greta had retrieved a second axe from an outhouse and had led the way to an area outside the paddock, where several tree trunks were stacked. She spent a few seconds sharpening the two axe blades with a whetstone, and then demonstrated to Betty how to sever the trunk by chopping a V-shape. At first, Betty found it hard to deliver the blade with both force and accuracy, but with words of encouragement from Greta each time she hit the target, she soon managed to get the knack of swinging the long-handled axe and guiding its path down. It took some minutes but eventually, her first log parted from its parent tree trunk. The exercise had raised Betty's heart rate and breathing. She was tempted to high-five Greta, but was not sure that the old woman would understand such a relatively modern gesture.

"Very good, child. Now we have to split the log. This time it is easier because we are slicing with the grain, instead of across it." Greta stood the log upright, and brought the axe down on the log, splitting it in two with the first stroke. Betty tried to copy, but her stroke embedded the axe in the half-log. "That's OK dear, now you have to lift the axe with the log stuck on it - it's heavier of course - and hit the log down on the ground as hard as you can." Betty followed the instruction. The combination was heavier to lift, but her second blow completed the split. Betty beamed with satisfaction.

"Right my child, we need quite a number of logs to keep us going through each day - here you see we have no shortage of timber." She waved her hand at the endless forest covering the mountains. "Indeed our homes are made mostly from timber. But I'm afraid I have been slightly devious with you. Wait here a moment." Greta walked over to the outbuilding, disappeared inside, and reappeared with a chain-saw in one hand and a safety helmet in the other. Betty laughed, but also felt some relief, as it would have taken hours of hard work for her to stockpile logs. "I just wanted you to understand the reality of life on the mountain, dear. When I was young, chopping was the way *all* the logs were made - humankind had worked with axes for centuries before the chain-saw arrived. Stand well back please."

Greta slipped the helmet and visor, over her head, and started the chain-saw with a pull on the starter rope. Betty stifled a giggle at the incongruous appearance of an old woman in a safety helmet, wielding such a noisy and dangerous weapon. Greta worked her way quickly along the tree trunk, taking only a few seconds to sever off each log.

"We still need to split some of them, mind," warned Greta. "I'll maybe teach you to use the chain-saw when your mind is functioning better, you have to have your wits about you using one of these."

"Oh, please teach me now Greta, I'm feeling much clearer after that hearty breakfast," begged Betty, not wanting to miss such an exciting opportunity.

Greta hesitated, looking at Betty searchingly. "Well, OK, my dear, but listen carefully…"

*   *   *

An hour later, well satisfied with the morning's work, they made several trips carrying the cut wood into the chalet, and stacked it near the fireplace and stove. Despite the cold weather, Betty found herself glowing with warmth after the exercise. "So do you go into the forest and cut the trees down yourself, Greta?" she asked.

"No my dear; it's not too difficult to cut down and debranch a tree, that's true, but to drag it out of the forest you need a vehicle. So, the foresters deliver me a pile of trunks, once in a while. Let's sit down with some coffee for a few minutes, then we can make some raclette for lunch"

"That would be lovely," replied Betty gratefully, "And then I should be on my way, I don't want to impose on your hospitality."

Greta looked surprised. "And where will you go?" she asked.

"Oh, well… I'm not sure yet," admitted Betty truthfully after a moment's contemplation.

"Well you can't just wander around in the snow again until you fall down with exhaustion," Greta castigated her. "Otto saved you last time, but you may not be so lucky next. I would be very happy to have you stay here with me until you have sorted your mind out. Besides, imagine how I would feel if you died in the snow a few kilometres on down the road."

"Oh dear, like Briccius," muttered Betty, remembering the historical story that George had related.

"Who's Briccius, dear?"

"Oh, he was a medieval knight who died in the snow. He thought he was carrying a vial of Christ's blood and tried to cross the Alps to evade his pursuers," explained Betty. Greta looked at her quizzically. "But the important thing is that I remembered it," insisted Betty. "Mostly I've been getting these feelings that I *nearly* remember something, though it just won't come. That's really frustrating, so it's satisfying when I actually do remember something."

"So how long ago did you learn about Briccius?" asked Greta.

"Mm… well, that was just last week, I think - I was on a skiing holiday with George."

"And can you remember other things about the skiing holiday?"

"Er, yes - there was a church where I played piano every morning. We stayed in a chalet. I remember the skiing, and celebrating New Year's Eve on the mountain."

"And do you remember things from before the holiday?" asked Greta.

"Yes." Betty scanned her memories. "I can remember home and work, and back in time to being a child. I can recall all of that OK."

"So it's just the last few days that are sketchy?"

"It seems so. What is the date today, Greta?"

"It's the 3rd of January dear."

"Right. So, after the New Year's celebration, I left Heiligenblut next morning. That's when the first kidnap attempt happened. Then we went to Villach with the police, and there was a blizzard that day, so we stayed in a Spa hotel for the night. We tried to fly home the next morning but the police wanted us back in Villach again. So that was the 2nd of January, just yesterday… though it feels like a long time ago." She ran her fingers through her hair, concentrating on trying to recall the sequence of events. "Yes, then George got ill - he had hurt his head in a fall during the blizzard, so we went to the hospital. We had a lovely police officer with us - Kathi - we talked a lot. And then we heard there had been another kidnap attempt. But then it all gets a bit hazy after that. I know we were aiming to leave early the following morning to get to the airport and home, but…" Betty grimaced as her efforts to recall further

114

came up blank.

"Relax, child. That's good. You only have half a day missing from your memory. Let's have some lunch and then you can try again."

Greta showed Betty how to slowly melt the cheese. "Keep stirring, and don't leave it standing on the stove too long at a time, else it might burn," she counselled.

Burn. The word was stirring up that same unrequited feeling in Betty's mind again. Burn. Burn. Ah, yes, Schweiger had come back to the hospital in the evening talking about burns on the crash victims. Betty smiled at Greta. "I just remembered a bit more, Greta." Then her smile faded as she remembered that Schweiger had been unwilling to let her leave the country, since he thought she was implicated in the kidnappers' deaths. But she did not bother Greta with those details.

$$* \qquad * \qquad *$$

After Betty woke from a post-lunch nap - the waves of sleepiness had still not completely abated - Greta put aside her sewing and suggested they go for a walk up the mountain track for some fresh air and exercise.

"About halfway up, you can get a phone signal, if you would like to let your family know you are safe."

"Oh, I don't want to risk turning my phone on, Greta. It might give away my location to those who would do me harm. In any case, the battery is flat."

"Well, put it on charge down there then." Greta gestured to one of the few electric sockets to be found in her chalet. "You can use my phone instead if you like."

"Oh, OK. Thanks."

"Now wrap up well - it gets colder as we gain height on the mountain."

Betty swung the overcoat over her ski jacket as they left.

"Yes, that's sensible dear. It's a lovely natural woollen coat, not like these modern synthetic materials. But it's very large - it looks more like a man's coat?" suggested Greta.

Betty looked down at it again and stroked the worsted material. There was something familiar about it that she could not quite place.

115

Something reassuring. "Yes it's what I was lying on in the kidnappers' van," she explained to Greta. "I just grabbed it round me when I made my getaway - it seemed so cold then." The two women started trudging through the snow round the back of the paddock to join Greta's mountain path, and started up a mild incline in single file. Betty, following, became acutely aware of Greta's grey hair, done up in a bun in front of her. The bun was agitating her memory again. Then it suddenly came back to her. She had done her own hair up in a bun so that she could impersonate a nurse, and get out of the hospital - and that's why she was wearing these scrubs under her outdoor clothes.

Otto mostly led, but occasionally disappeared into the trees, examining something of canine interest. They trudged on in silence apart from the sound of their boots compacting the snow, and Betty focussed on trying to remember parts of the walkabout she had made from the hospital. The bundle of wet clothes, the initial fear, and then the man; the man whom she had liked, even though he had ridiculed her idea of escape, and who had led her to a launderette and they had eaten together in a restaurant - goulash. And he had persuaded her to return to the hospital. Stuart - that was his name. Well, actually it wasn't. She smiled at the recollection of his supportive manner, and the playfulness of his conversation. Ah, and it was *he* that wore this overcoat. So how did she now have it? She tried to remember if he had given it to her. No, she recalled him still wearing it when they had said goodbye - she had affectionately tugged at the lapel as she reached up to kiss him briefly. Now the events were all coming back to her. And Lukas the police guard had been cross with her when she returned. Then Taube had visited with the Romanian phone number, and she had called Tom Wheatley to talk it over. Then came the painstaking hours of programming work on her phone to extend the weapon capability of her phone by hacking a caller's location. After that, she had slept but been woken by Wheatley phoning to check she was OK. And then George had been a nuisance not letting her sleep further. But try as she might, she could not remember further than that, or indeed recall clearly what George had actually said or done to make her feel so negatively about him. It felt rather sour that the end-point of what she could remember of yesterday, was feeling resentful of George's presence. Then she wondered guiltily if it had something to do with meeting Stuart, to whom she had definitely felt an attraction.

They had reached a small plateau on the side of the mountain, and Greta, using the advantage of the height they had gained, was pointing out local landmarks. A solitary and long off-piste run down the Stadlerbach mountain on the opposite side of the valley, which she had skied as a child, long before a ski-lift was built to access it from the other side. And a flour mill on the river, which had been powered by a water wheel in Greta's younger days but which, she stated wistfully, though not bitterly, now used electricity. Betty was hot from the exertion of the uphill walk and opened the front of the large overcoat, allowing it to billow out behind her. A broken cloud layer partly shrouded the mountains opposite, rolling like transient, loosely hung veils, in a pattern never to be exactly repeated, defying the comparative permanence of those mountain peaks. Betty, listening to the way Greta talked, glimpsed some of the charming reality and depth of knowledge that comes from living a whole life in one particular mountain region.

"So my dear, if you are happy to walk further, there is a spot, about a kilometre on, where we can get a cell phone signal - it's where I go when I want to chat to my children." Betty nodded and smiled. It was indeed delightful and humbling to find that an old woman was prepared to walk two kilometres up a mountain in snow, just to be able to talk for a few minutes with her grown children on her phone. But clearly, Greta had lived like this, or harder, all her life - she thought nothing of hiking and chopping, fulfilling a daily round of essential jobs. A simple life, but an honourable, healthy and rewarding one, for which Betty felt admiration and respect.

They trekked onwards and upwards again, Betty's attention returning again to the reconstruction of her memories of the day before. But though she repeatedly tried, she could progress events no further than the feeling of resentment against George. So, she turned to considering the logic of her situation. Clearly, she had been kidnapped somehow, but had escaped. But why was she lying on Stuart's coat in the back of the kidnappers' van? Had she seen Stuart again that night, and he had given it to her? - she had no recollection of such an event. Or had the kidnappers taken it from him somehow? But he had not been at the hospital, assuming that was where she had been taken from. Had he tried to intervene? And why was she in Switzerland, west from Austria, instead of halfway to the Black Sea, to the East? Then the horror of the connection came to her. Had it been *Stuart* driving the van - taking her west towards home? Was she lying on his coat because he had put it there for her? Had she killed Stuart, instead of the kidnappers? She stopped in her tracks, frozen by the thought, and feeling rather nauseous. Greta didn't notice for a few seconds. Then she turned, presumably missing the sound of Betty's boots on the snow behind her.

"Are you OK my dear," she asked with concern. "Are you feeling weak again?" She hurried back to where Betty was standing, leaning forward, clutching her stomach.

"Oh, I'm sorry Greta. I've been remembering more, and I've just reached a horrible realisation."

"Tell me, child."

"Oh, no I don't want to bother you with the details Greta, it's OK."

"Nonsense. I may be just a simple old woman, but I understand life, I am here to listen and to help you." Greta put her arm around Betty, the same way she had to help her walk when they first met.

"Well, I can remember up to a certain point yesterday evening, but then my memory just seems to stop. Then the first thing I remember *after* that, is waking up in the back of a van, this morning, as I told you. When the van stopped, I used a weapon on the driver - I couldn't see him, but I think I must have killed him and then I ran away. But now I remember whose overcoat this is - a good man - and I think... You see I was lying on this coat in the van... And I was being taken west, not east as the kidnappers would have headed... So I am thinking maybe it was that good man who was driving, and not the kidnappers. I think I have killed a friend... by mistake. Betty doubled over and howls of grief rose from her belly to be cried out through an aching throat. Greta held onto her and tears of sympathy welled in her eyes also. They stood like that for a few minutes while Betty cried herself out. Betty also reconnected with the last time she had cried, in the car, at the beginning of her journey to the assisted suicide, when things were still simple, though heart-rending, before all this kidnapping craziness had started.

"Shall we go back, now, child?"

"No, Greta, let's go on, I think better when I am walking, and then you can still phone your children."

They started on upwards again. At first, Greta looked back every few seconds to check on Betty. Maybe it was the chilling thoughts, or maybe the wind was slightly stronger on this part of the track, but suddenly Betty was feeling very cold. The overcoat was billowing, unbuttoned, behind her. She pulled it back around her again. Somehow, it seemed wrong to get comfort from a dead man's coat, but it did comfort her. Indeed, it was the only thing she had to remember him by - a man that she had briefly liked, so much. She started sobbing again.

"No Greta, keep going, really," she urged to the worried woman.

118

Betty wiped her face unceremoniously on the sleeve of the woollen coat. The cold wind was making the tears icily painful. They trudged on. Eventually, the track flattened into a plateau, devoid of trees, with a commanding view across the valley.

"We are here," announced Greta, and she fumbled down into a deep inside pocket for the cell phone, which she clearly treasured, although she could only use it after an arduous climb. "You have to keep a phone in a warm place - the battery goes flat quickly in this cold. Do you know that dear?"

"Yes, I know that, Greta." Betty smiled at her, enjoying the woman's naive but cherishing appreciation of a small piece of modern technology.

"Would you like to use it first?" offered Greta.

"Actually no, I dare not, Greta. You see, any call I make would likely enable people to trace me to here, and I would rather stay safe and on my own, until I have worked out what to do. The Austrian police want me for questioning, though I have done nothing wrong, and my own people will pursue me for killing the man who owned this coat, even though it was a mistake." She sobbed again. "And I still don't understand how the kidnappers keep tracing my whereabouts. So please don't say anything about me during your phone calls, even to your family. I'll have a look around at the views so you can have some privacy." Betty strode off to one side of the clearing. The view was stunning and the air so fresh that she felt somewhat cleansed of the guilt in which she had wallowed on the walk up. She could see Greta's little chalet, far below, a wisp of smoke rising from its chimney - the fire still burning up the logs that she had helped to prepare. She looked back at Greta, the old woman's face lit up with joy at talking with her family. Then she walked over to the other side of the clearing. There was a sheer precipice over the edge. She shuddered, remembering the hairpin bend over which the kidnap van had crashed. Then she remembered the moments before that, when she had been determined to follow through with a comfortable suicide. It had seemed like a sensible decision then - a celebration of life well lived and a refusal to compromise it in the future. Perhaps it didn't need to be comfortable. She took a step toward the precipice. Perhaps it was even more sensible now - a solution also to all this complex mess and guilt that she had got herself into. She edged forward a little more. Otto had walked over to her and made a low anxious whine. She could just about see where she would land - it was very far down. Surely, that would just be the end. The feeling of vertigo was very strong. But what about Greta - it would be so unkind to do this in front of her.

Fundamentally though, it was still the best solution, perhaps even more so now. But then she remembered that she was already in Switzerland. Surely, she could easily get to the clinic in Zurich from here?

Decisively she turned away from the precipice, glancing back at Greta who was still absorbed in conversation, and walked across to the other side with the view down to Greta's home. It was too cold to stand still so she paced whilst watching the clouds roll over the peaks. Greta had now finished her chat and joined Betty.

"We should go back now before it begins to get dark. My family are all well - Don't worry dear, I said nothing about you being here. Now, the walk down is not so much effort as the walk up, but it is a bit more tricky. Try to walk a little bit sideways on the steeper parts - as if you were skiing, so as not to slip. Perhaps I should have got out the snowshoes. How are you feeling now, dear?"

"I'm feeling a bit clearer, still a bit sad and shocked, but I have a plan now." Greta smiled at her approvingly, and led the way back down.

*   *   *

Greta cooked a traditional Swiss Lil'Luna for their supper - Betty ate heartily but decided she did not want to ask where the chicken had come from. And then Greta served a Gebrannte Crème for dessert - she would not let Betty help with that as she said that it was important to get the caramelising of the sugar perfect, otherwise it would taste burnt. Then, after washing up, the two sat down by the fire and talked, Otto lying by Greta's chair. The sun had long since set, and the light from the hearth fire was supplemented by a single candle.

"Greta, I have decided on the best plan to sort out my problems, and it involves getting to Zurich," - she was not more explicit with the details. "How would I do that from here?"

"That's easy, child. You can catch a bus on the main road that you walked here from - the bus goes through Davos and then on to Zurich - it takes about two hours. I know because I have very occasionally visited my daughter there. I do find the city rather overwhelming, but I confess I enjoy the bus ride, looking at all the different places from the window."

"Oh," Betty was delighted to hear that it was not so far. "And do they accept Euros on the bus? I confess I think I bribed the driver on the way here, but it was accidental because I didn't know which country I was in." She laughed at the vague memory. "Although I am not certain that I was actually in Switzerland when I boarded the bus - I really have little idea how long I was on the bus for."

"I think you must have already been in Switzerland, my dear, there are no buses around here which cross a border, as far as I am aware. But no, you need to pay the driver in Swiss francs. Don't worry, I can give you enough francs - the fare is only about 40. I keep plenty of cash here because it is rare I can be bothered to go all the way into Davos to visit a bank."

"Oh, thank you again, Greta. I will give you Euros to cover it - in fact, I must give you some money for my stay - to cover the food and things."

"No, I won't hear of it, my dear. You have been my guest, and it has been a delight to have you here - I see so few people during the winter months. To be honest I will be sad to see you go. No, just give me Euros to cover the fare. That is good."

"Is there a bus tomorrow?"

"Yes, my dear," Greta laughed, "there are lots of buses tomorrow - life may be simple and remote here, but we are well connected to civilisation. After breakfast, I will walk with you back to the main road to see you onto the 10 o'clock bus. I want to make sure you don't collapse again, like this morning. But considering our walk up the mountain this afternoon, I would say you seem fit again. Does that suit you?"

"Yes, that suits me perfectly Greta. What would I have done without you?"

"Without *Otto* and me," Greta reminded her. "Would you like to listen to some music before we sleep? I'm afraid I have no TV or anything like that, but my son loaded lots of music into my phone and gave me a little speaker that I can plug it into. I don't quite understand how it all works - these tiny mobile phones are amazing things."

"More than you know," muttered Betty cryptically.

"Would you like to choose the music?" Greta handed the phone to Betty.

"OK. If you had a piano, I would play to you. But I'll see if I can find some piano music." She knelt down by the speaker and plugged it in. Then she scanned the directory. "Wow, your son really has loaded a lot for you."

"Yes, I can't understand how it all fits inside such a small device." Greta shook her head and Betty laughed.

"Ah, here is my favourite - Enescu's Adagio." She started it playing and sat in front of the hearth. It wasn't long before the tears started - the poignancy of the music reminding her again of her suicide decision.

"It's a very sad piece, dear. But very beautiful."

"Yes. Sorry, that was silly. I shouldn't have played such a heart-rending work. Let's try… this. I actually played this just the evening before last, on an exquisite Grand piano in a hotel in Warmbaderhof - it's Liszt." They settled back in the glow of the fire, listening to the flow of the music. Finally, Betty retired off to the spare bed, after Greta showed her how to stack logs into the fire to keep it going for the night.

*   *   *

Chapter 7
To Zurich

Betty woke in the morning to the sound of the hens outside clucking enthusiastically. She stretched, feeling very refreshed. She deduced that it must be the hens' feeding time, and smiled at the recollection of the hens' simple earnestness. But the smile dissipated as the worries of her situation and the terrible knowledge of what she had unwittingly done to Stuart, re-established themselves as dominant in her waking mind. Still, she reasoned to herself, she had planned a resolution, a way out, and today was the trip to Zurich.

A little later, after freshening up, she joined Greta, who was outside, now cutting logs to keep her stock high. "Good morning, child, did you sleep well?" she asked between blows with the axe. Betty breathed in the cold clean mountain air. "I hope I didn't wake you - I wanted to make an early start so that I can give you breakfast and stack the fire, before we trek down the valley to the main road."

"I feel great Greta, thanks - well physically anyway," Betty smiled. "Do you want a hand?"

"No, dear. You save your strength for the walk. I'm almost done - just a couple more logs will be enough for today. I think there will be more snow later, so I'd rather get it done this morning. I've already milked the goats."

*   *   *

After breakfast, Greta organised herself for the walk. Betty looked around the tiny chalet wistfully. Greta noticed. "You arrived with nothing, child, so you leave nothing behind."

123

"Well I hope I leave some friendship behind," commented Betty. "Perhaps I will write to you sometimes." Then she wished she hadn't said it, as she remembered that her plan did not allow for 'sometimes', and the tears came to her eyes yet again.

Greta came over and hugged her. "Dear child, such worries... such troubles. Now you have your francs safe for the bus? And did you remember to put your phone in an inside pocket, otherwise that battery will go flat again?"

"Yes, Greta." Betty humoured her - it was comforting to be mothered. But she had been more than careful *not* to turn the phone on - in fact, she had wondered if she would ever use it again.

The trek back along the valley was uneventful - they saw no one and passed no vehicles - the valley was truly remote. Betty felt she could not have stumbled upon a better place to hide away. About halfway, it began to snow lightly. Greta dismissed the idea that she should head back, insisting that she was quite used to walking, snow or no snow. Otto mostly trotted along with them, just occasionally delving off to one side or the other for an investigation. It seemed quite far, and Betty was impressed by the distance that, in desperation, she had managed to walk, the previous day. At length, they met the main road, and Greta showed Betty where they should wait for the bus, putting Otto back on his lead for safety. Occasional cars now passed, and Betty felt a little anxious about whether she might still be being searched for. Indeed she was wearing the same clothes that she had the previous day - she had nothing to change into - the last she had seen of her own clothes they were still drying on the hospital room radiators.

"Thank you so much for everything, Greta." Betty hugged Greta as the bus appeared in the distance. "You have helped a lot, in so many ways." She bent over and ruffled Otto's head. "And you found me, Otto, when I was half-dead, and saved me. Thank you too."

"I will think of you often, child. Take care, and remember the simple things in life." Greta held out her arm to signal the bus to stop. A man stepped off the bus carrying some bags of produce. He clearly recognised Greta and stopped to chat. "Good morning Frau Schrödinger, how are you?"

Betty stepped onto the bus and managed a greeting in German for the driver, telling him her destination was Zurich, and paying him with her precious Swiss francs. She found a seat and sat down, waving back to Greta as the bus pulled away. Then she burst into tears again, but kept it quiet so as not to be noticed by the other passengers. After a few minutes, she dried her eyes on the coat sleeve once more, and started watching the white snow-covered countryside roll by as she reconsidered her situation. She was certain that she was safe on the bus, and should also be safe in the anonymity of a large city like Zurich. But she had no more Swiss francs, and she knew that the moment she used her credit card, the UK authorities, at least, would be on her trail. She recalled the time, about a year ago when she previously visited Dignitas and discussed her looming illness and her wishes, with them. So, she had already supplied them then, with the paperwork and medical evidence that they needed. The appointment she had arranged for two days ago had been missed of course, but she was sure that probably happened often, and they would be accommodating. What she felt unsure about was how quickly they would be willing to proceed - they had, she knew, very strict protocols about more than one meeting, with time for reflection following each. Anyway, she decided, she would go straight there and start the ball rolling. Perhaps first, she wondered, she should withdraw some Swiss francs with her credit card on the opposite side of Zurich. No, she would go to Dignitas first so that she knew where she stood.

Having decided her immediate plan, Betty relaxed and watched the groups of skiers getting on and off around Davos and Klosters, before the bus proceeded through more countryside. Once or twice, she made another attempt to see if she could progress her memory beyond the block that she had reached, but to no avail. And once or twice, she started to review her whole life in an attempt to commemorate it before the end, but each time she found the process too painful and gave up on it as indulgent. She even felt safe enough in the bus to doze a little.

But finally, the bus was wending through the outskirts of the city and into the bus station. Betty decided she would be last off the bus, for no particular reason. As she tried to merge in with the crowds, she felt a bit conspicuous. She had no luggage, and she felt somewhat untidily dressed in comparison to those in the vicinity, with the oversized overcoat bundled around her, and nearly reaching her feet. She thought about abandoning the overcoat and relying on her ski jacket, but then her scrubs would be visible. Anyway, she loved the overcoat - it had served her well and in some way, it gave her a connection to Stuart's memory, which she valued and, strangely, felt a duty toward. She found a taxi and told him the address she wanted. Taxi drivers were pragmatic - he would accept euros at the end.

It cost her an extra five on top of the fare. But she had quite a stash of euros - she had found a further liberal supply in one of Stuart's overcoat pockets. As she stepped out of the taxi, the snow had all but stopped. The blanket of grey cloud that had obscured most of the sky, most of the morning, was showing signs of beginning to break up, with a silver lining round the edge of the cloud obscuring where the sun would have been.

*   *   *

She strode into the Dignitas reception and explained, apologised, that she had missed an appointment two days ago for inescapable reasons and would they be kind enough to reschedule her, for today, if that was possible? As she spoke, she wondered ruefully if 'inescapable reasons' was the right phrase to use - what do you say when you are detained by the police and then kidnapped? But the receptionist was warm and reassuring and took her name.

"Ah, yes... Miss Gosmore. We had a gentleman in here yesterday asking if you had visited, and he requested that we let him know immediately if you arrived. He said he was from the British Embassy, and it was very urgent that he speak with you." Betty felt panic rising. "But of course it is entirely up to you," she went on, "whether we do actually let him know - we would never betray someone's privacy," she continued in a hushed tone sensing Betty's sudden unease.

"Oh, no... no, please do not tell him, or anyone else, that I am here. He probably is not who he claims to be - I have had some trouble..."

"That's perfectly OK, Miss Gosmore, your visits here are completely confidential. Would you like to wait in that private room over there, to the right, whilst I see if I can arrange for a counsellor to see you."

Betty thanked her, and walked across into the private room that the receptionist had indicated. Betty sat rather shakily into a chair. She had not expected that. No one was supposed to know she was coming here. How the hell had they found out? - Oh god, of course, she had told Stuart, and he would have told Wheatley. Wheatley might have told the police. Shit! *and* her old phone calls had been hacked by the kidnappers so they knew as well. Everybody knew there was a chance she would show up here! Nevertheless, it would be OK as long as the receptionist was sincere. However, visions of secret agents quietly handing over wads of money to the receptionist, and promising more if she fed them information, were appearing in Betty's alarmed mind. This was a disaster - perhaps she should leave now? Or perhaps she could ask if the counsellor would talk to her somewhere else? And if the kidnappers did get to her again, her only weapon was compromised - if she turned her phone on, to enable it to be used, then her whereabouts would immediately be revealed to Wheatley. No, wait a minute, if she bought a new SIM card with a new number, then the phone would be incognito, and she would still have her weapon app. Yes! That would solve one half of the problem…

The jumble of alarmed thoughts was interrupted by a young woman entering the room, and closing the door behind her. "Hello Miss Gosmore, my name is Mila Klausman, I am one of the counsellors here. It's good to meet you." She held out her hand in greeting, with a smile that seemed modest and genuine, rather than staged for the occasion. Betty stood to shake her hand and was calmed by her confident but caring manner. Betty again felt scruffily dressed, at least compared with this woman, whose hair was woven into an immaculate curl of Dutch braid, and whose grey business dress was smart without being showy. "Nina, on reception, said you were concerned that someone had asked here for you?" She sat and gestured to Betty to do the same.

"Yes, I have had some troubles the last couple of days, which incidentally caused me to miss my original appointment - sorry, and anyone trying to find me, at the moment, is likely to be a threat. They might even try bribing for information."

"OK, well don't worry on that score - we will not give out any information to anyone asking - as you know we operate on very high standards of ethics and we take our clients' privacy very seriously. And I assure you," she laughed gently, "Nina is incorruptible. Would you like to take your coat off?" She gestured to Betty's enormous overcoat that was still draped around her.

"Oh, yes. It is quite warm in here." Betty pulled off the coat, laid it on the chair next to her, and unzipped her ski jacket. "I apologise," she muttered, embarrassed to reveal the scrubs, "about my appearance - the last couple of days have been very difficult." Betty made a mental note that she needed to buy some new clothes as soon as possible.

"There's no need to apologise," Mila reassured her. "Do you want to talk about those difficulties you have had the last couple of days?" Mila asked directly.

"Oh, no, thanks for your concern, but those issues I can deal with myself."

"So," continued Mila, gesturing to the file that she had placed on the table, "I have read through the discussion and paperwork you had with one of my colleagues when you visited us here last - has the situation changed?"

"Unfortunately yes… or inevitably yes, the symptoms have now started, so I want to progress my plan to end my life." Betty's voice cracked slightly on the last few words.

"I understand," Mila nodded. "So, first we need to make sure you understand all the context in which you make your decision. Importantly, are you aware that there has just recently been published the results of a Phase I/II trial of a new possible treatment for Huntington's disease? It's not like the traditional drugs that just damp down movements - this involves antisense RNA, which in effect silences the gene, so theoretically preventing progression of the disease. Both the safety and the effectiveness have been reported as very promising."

Betty, amazed, was sitting quite motionless with her mouth slightly open. A break in the clouds finally allowed a bright shaft of sunlight to track through the window, across the file which Mila had placed on the table, and onto the overcoat next to Betty.

"What! How could I have missed that?" gasped Betty. "I am such a fool. I am supposed to be a savvy scientist…"

Mila smiled. "The research paper was published just a couple of weeks ago, in the run-up to Christmas so I guess it didn't get a lot of publicity. Would you like me to print out a copy of the research article for you to read?"

"Please," nodded Betty.

"So, it is what it is," said Mila standing. "A research trial. It is not for me to raise your hopes or otherwise. I believe they are now actively expanding the trial. You must make your own judgements. I will go and print a copy for you - I'll be back in a couple of minutes." She left the room and closed the door behind her.

Betty felt a serene lightness and emptiness, an almost absence of thoughts. A shock, but a very benign shock, that not only made her immediate plan redundant, but instantiated a future, which she had never expected to have. Betty had always lived never expecting to get middle-aged or old, never expecting to have children, always just living a Peter

Pan life, not overly concerned with responsibilities. Now an additional dimension was being added to her life… maybe. Too late for my father, she couldn't help thinking, but he would be overjoyed for me. That made her eyes mist over again, not for the first time that day.

Mila returned after a couple of minutes and handed to Betty a thin sheaf of clipped A4 paper. "So I imagine you will want to read and digest this before talking to me any further? You can contact us any time again, but only if you want to, of course."

Betty thanked her, and aware of the greater chance of being discovered at the clinic the longer she stayed, decided to leave as soon as possible. Nina phoned a taxi for her - she would have caught the tram back into the city centre, but again had no Swiss francs. She folded the report and stuffed it in the inside breast pocket of the overcoat, which she pulled close to her, as she left. A furtive look around revealed no one obviously watching the clinic entrance, though she could not be certain if anyone was sitting in any of the cars parked nearby.

During the taxi ride she tried to strike a new plan - a 'Bureau de change' must be one of her first stops, then some new clothes and a hotel. Much depended on how many euros she actually had. Sitting in the back of the cab, she stealthily pulled out the stash of notes that she had found in Stuart's overcoat and counted them, adding in her own, out of sight of the taxi driver. 687 euros all together - enough for clothes, a new SIM card, toiletries and a few nights in a hotel, without using her credit card. Perfect - she needed time to think things through, to work out what to do longer term. She pulled out the paper bag of sandwiches that Greta had kindly insisted she take, and made a lunch of them. She was still feeling some anxiety about possibly being followed from Dignitas, so she got the taxi driver to drop her in a busy shopping area on a main road where there was no parking. That would make it difficult for any driver following. She thrust the fare into the taxi driver's hand and bolted out of the cab, down a side street, and round a corner, glancing back at each turn to check if anyone was running behind. There was no one obviously following - she felt relatively safe and set about looking for somewhere to change her money into local currency.

*   *   *

That done, with a fat bundle of Swiss francs safely stashed in an inside-pocket, she made a quick stop to buy a stamp and a 'Thank You' card, which she intended for Greta. Next, she found a phone shop and bought a new prepaid SIM card that she immediately inserted into her phone. She could now turn it on without fear of being tracked. She sat in the phone shop for a while and checked that she could again run her special zap app - the green indicator telling her that the equipment back at GCHQ was indeed all charged up and ready to use, should she need it. That boosted her confidence. Then she googled hotels in the local area - wincing at some of the Swiss prices, but finding one or two that suited her. Finally, she searched for fashionable clothes shops nearby, and headed off to find replacements for the 'scrubs and overcoat' image. She spent rather more than she was comfortable with, on a new outfit. Though she would have been happier to shower before putting on the new clothes, she decided to change into them then and there, top them with her ski jacket with the hood up, and put Stuart's overcoat into the bag. That way, she considered that when she walked out of the shop, her appearance would be so radically changed that it would further confuse anyone who still might be attempting to follow her. Thus disguised, she headed for the Hotel Alexander. It was situated in a busy, pedestrianised area that she considered gave her a degree of protection against being abducted in a vehicle. She still could not shake off that nagging anxiety of being vulnerable.

Once in her hotel room, she luxuriated in a long hot shower, so welcome after one night spent on the hospital floor and van, and another at Greta's where she had only been able to use a kettle-full of hot water in a bowl for washing, much as she valued the latter as a learning experience. Then she sat and read through the research paper on RNA antisense treatment of Huntington's disease that Mila had printed for her. She read it in detail a second time, concluding that it did indeed seem credible and very encouraging. And so with some optimism, she started to consider what her longer-term plan should be.

The choice seemed to be between returning to the UK or staying invisible abroad. She could contact Tom Wheatley to help her get back to the UK, and then face the difficulties about having murdered Stuart. She would hope the authorities would understand that it had been an accident, but she would also have to explain why and how she had a weapon, derived from GCHQ research, but unknown to them. Or, on the other hand, she could try to remain invisible, perhaps staying in Zurich, and starting a new life here. She would have to get some sort of job, without paperwork, and fast - life was expensive in Switzerland. She reasoned that perhaps she could maybe get cash in hand giving piano lessons. To that end, she searched in google maps for piano shops, and was intrigued to find one called 'Kindermusikladen bei Musik hug', which seemed to her to translate as 'Children's music store : Music Hug' - this might be just the place for piano lessons, and it was just a few doors down from the 'Steinway Piano Gallery' which might also be a possibility for a job. They were only a few minutes walk away, so she decided to make a visit straight away whilst the idea was still hot.

She strode down the wide promenade between the trams and the River Limmat, feeling much more confident now that she was washed and well dressed, and enjoying the views of the bridges and buildings, glorified intermittently by late afternoon sunshine. She reached the Steinway Piano Gallery first. It was as impressive as it sounded, with arrays of grand pianos, mostly black, one white and one lacquered wood, lined up in rows with their lids open like ranks of soldiers saluting. There were a couple of people looking at a piano at the far end. Betty felt the thrill of delight inside that she always got from pianos, and it was not difficult to engage the salesperson in some technical discussion about how soundboards differ in Steinway from other pianos, letting her enthusiasm and knowledge shine through. He invited her to try one of the pianos and she gratefully sat and stilled herself. She needed this to be impressive, so she chose a lesser-known Chopin study, composed to show off technique and launched into it, savouring the sound of the pristine instrument, and soon losing herself in the music. A few minutes in, however, but fortunately during a slow passage, a potential disaster struck - her right hand was momentarily taken over by one of the involuntary jerks - it grazed a couple of black notes and the heel of her palm landed on three adjacent white notes. It was a difficult combination to rationalise musically, but she kept her cool, improvising heavily, to reconstruct and deconstruct that errant phrase in a discordant contemporary style, until she had woven it into the music in an apparently meaningful way. Then gradually she modulated her keys back to where she had been before the intrusion, and continued, concluding the study without any further problem. Betty was satisfied that she had done a masterful job of disguising the intrusion - to someone who didn't know the study, it would have sounded like a sudden, unusual but interesting mid-passage.

She re-engaged the salesperson in conversation about details of the tone of the instrument and the acoustics of the room, dropping in a hint that she was looking for work. The hint was not picked up though, so eventually, she asked directly if there was any possibility of employment there. She was politely told that there was no vacancy at the moment, but he gave her quite a lot of information about the music scene in Zurich.

Betty walked on down the street to the Children's music shop. It was a surprisingly large store, stocking all types of instruments as well as pianos. All the staff seemed to be busy, so she wandered to an available piano and started to play some jocular music that she remembered entertaining her young niece with some months before. Indeed, she got the attention of a couple of young girls who were obviously bored whilst their parents were engaged in conversation with one of the store staff. She exaggerated her hand movements and made faces to the music which elicited some giggles and smiles. But it seemed the parents were intent on getting a small violin for one of the children rather than a piano. Eventually, Betty got to ask the salesperson if there was any demand for piano lessons, and was shown a notice board where several musicians were offering lessons on various instruments including piano. Betty was invited to pin a notice with her details there - Betty expressed thanks and said she would think about it.

She walked back to the river and leaned over the railings, watching the lights reflecting and flickering in the water, with mixed feelings. She felt refreshed, as she always did, from having spent some time playing on a piano. However, it looked as if the idea of quickly finding a job that would support her in Zurich, was overly ambitious. If she wanted to avoid using her credit card, and that itself had a limited supply of funds anyway, the only other option for getting money here would be for her to phone her mother. But Betty was fairly certain that the UK authorities would easily trace her if she did that.

But then she wondered if there was really any point in trying to evade the UK authorities by staying in Zurich? It wasn't as if it would change the fact of what she had done - she would still have to live with the feelings of having killed Stuart accidentally. And it seemed unlikely that the UK authorities would lock her up for that - perhaps it would be better to contact Tom Wheatley, be honest about what had happened and hope he would help her get home, without the Austrian police badgering her further. It would certainly be easier for her to get onto the Huntington's research treatment program back in the UK, where she had access to her medical paperwork, and that too was urgent. She resolved to put off making the fateful decision until tomorrow - tonight she would go to the Zurich Opera House. One of the flyers in the music shop had advertised that this evening there was a performance of 'La Bohème' - too good to miss.

Betty visited a restaurant for a meal. It was the first food she had eaten since Greta's wholesome plain meals, and though the restaurant food was good, she felt slightly nostalgic for the rustic life. She arrived at the Opera House early, wanting to savour the atmosphere of the building. After walking around and appreciating the neo-classical external façade for a few minutes, she went inside to the box office. There were very few tickets still remaining, but she managed to get a single seat in the front of the third circle, though at a price which threatened to further restrict the longevity of any stay in Zurich. Able to leave her ski-jacket in the cloakroom, she felt equal to mingling with Swiss high society in her new outfit. After taking in the luxury of the ladies' restroom, she wandered around the corridors for a while before finding her seat in the auditorium. The interior was stunning. She gratefully drank in the neo-rococo décor, resplendent in gold, and the extravagant paintings on the ceiling surrounding a massive chandelier, before looking down to watch the audience arriving in the stalls below.

Betty was enraptured by the performance itself, being drawn into the characters comprising the story. When the tragic final scene drew to a close, there was a brief respectful silence as the echoes of the music died away, and then, massive applause, of an enthusiasm only experienced at operas.

Walking out and back along the riverside again, Betty ruminated on the operatic story, but finding, ironically, that in many ways, it was the antithesis of her own situation. Mimi dies of her illness, whereas Betty now had hope of a reprieve; Colline pawns his overcoat to buy medicine for Mimi, whereas Betty had been profligate with the money she had found in someone else's overcoat. But she smiled, savouring the remembered echoes of the performance, and was determined not to feel chastened - this was, after all, the 21st century, not the bohemians' Paris of the 19th century. She should live her life the best way she could, as she had always done, except that the dark shadow of what she had done to Stuart, albeit inadvertently, would hang over her forever.

* * *

THURSDAY 5th January

When Betty awoke the next morning, she resolved that she would make a decision about her future after she had showered and breakfasted, although in truth she already knew what that decision would be. She finally sat down with a cup of coffee to think it all through and plan what to do. It was now obvious to her that to try to build a new life without access to authorities for paperwork, and without contact with friends and family, was not practicable. She knew that the first step was to phone Tom Wheatley at MI5, not least because her passport was still with the Austrian police and so she needed help from the establishment to get home to the UK. He had always sounded warm and reassuring on previous calls, but she was dreading the inevitable discussion about Stuart's death, and wondering whether his attitude might have completely changed. She decided to hedge her bets slightly by calling him from a public phone booth, and then if the conversation did not turn out well, she would at least only have betrayed her whereabouts to the city of Zurich - he would still not be able to track her movements on her cell phone. But Betty had seen no phone booth on her walks around Zurich, and her online search efforts only revealed that the Swiss telecoms company had been given permission to remove them all due to lack of usage. However, the article ended by saying that the last phone booth ever would probably be at a railway station - so it seemed like a reasonable idea to visit the central Zurich railway station - it was not far to walk.

When she got there, she traipsed around the massive station searching - but no signs to 'Telephones'. After asking a couple of people she was eventually told to look right down at the end of the lockers, and indeed, there they were - a block of six smart glass kiosks, all completely empty. She chose one, walked inside, took a deep breath, and phoned Tom Wheatley's number.

She was rather startled when a woman's voice answered, "Hello?" - had she misremembered Wheatley's number - was she stranded?

"Uhm, is Tom Wheatley there please?"

"Who is this speaking please?"

"It's Betty Gosmore."

"Yes, wait a moment please."

That sounded more positive. As she waited she realised she would not have been stranded anyway - she would still have Wheatley's number in her mobile phone.

"Hello Betty, Are you OK? Where are you?" It was that warm, comforting voice of Wheatley's, albeit sounding a little shriller than usual.

"Ah, Hi Tom. Yes, I'm fine - I'm at Zurich railway station."

"Zurich! Well, I can't tell you how happy I am to hear from you - we have been frantic the last couple of days. We weren't sure whether you had been taken again, or gone off on your own or had an accident... Why didn't you contact us?"

Betty felt some guilt at having caused them concern.

"I'm sorry Tom. I was very confused after what happened. I needed some time to sort things out."

"Of course, no, no, it's us who should be sorry - we failed to look after you. And they gave you a heavy dose of that tranquilliser - Stuart said you were still out for hours after he rescued you. But, we were guessing that perhaps you didn't know that he had rescued you?"

"Well, that's right, Tom. I certainly didn't know at the time - but, to be honest I did work it out some hours later."

"So are you feeling OK now, after the drug I mean?

"Oh, well, sort of. The physical effects have worn off, but I still can't remember anything that happened that night - it's just a blank."

"Yes, it's not surprising - it's an effect of that drug - that's one of the reasons they use it. But don't worry. Apart from the immediate period of memory loss, there are no other lasting effects - and we'll get you medically checked over when you get back. Oh..." His voice changed as he remembered Betty's original plan. "Or were you planning to visit Dignitas there?"

"OK, well listen Tom, I did already visit Dignitas, but I found out from them that there is a new treatment for my condition, so, fortunately, I have been able to put aside that course of action, at least for the foreseeable future."

"Ah." His voice sounded genuinely pleased. "That is good news, Betty. I am very pleased for you. So can we talk about getting you back to the UK?"

"Yes, the problem is the Austrian police are still holding my passport."

"No, they aren't. I have that here. After the farce at the hospital, the police were so embarrassed at their incompetent protection that they express couriered everything I asked for, to me here - your luggage and old phone and those important photographs - I got that all yesterday. So I'll courier your passport now, to you at your hotel - can you be there tomorrow morning to sign for it?"

"Yes, OK. It's the Alexander Hotel, Niederdorfstrasse."

"And then let me know what flight you'll be on and I'll meet you at the airport?"

"Well, yes. But what sort of trouble will I be in Tom?"

"Trouble. What do you mean? Why would you be in trouble, Betty?"

Why was he being so circumspect? "Well," Betty's voice trembled as she struggled to say it. "For accidentally killing Stuart - I'm so sorry, Tom, I honestly had no idea it was him in the van - I thought it was the kidnappers driving... I'm so sorry..."

"What... You thought you had killed Stuart?... No, no, Stuart is fine - actually, you did hurt his pride - I'm not sure he'll ever recover from that." Wheatley laughed. "No, he got back from buying some food and coffee at the truck stop and found the cab had been messed with - the steering wheel was broken through and the ignition wouldn't work, and when he looked into the back of the van, you were gone. He searched everywhere around the truck stop of course, but couldn't do much more until he got a new vehicle. We weren't sure whether the kidnappers had re-taken you or whether you had bolted of your own accord because you thought they still had you, and perhaps used this fictional laser-gun on the cab of the van - pretty neat actually." Then he realised. "Oh but I'm sorry - you must have felt awful if you thought you had clobbered Stuart?"

In answer, Betty just burst into tears.

*   *   *

A few hours later found Betty wandering back along to the Hotel, having been making the most of her last day in Zurich. Approaching the door, she realised that the man rising from a seat close by, to greet her, was Stuart. A flurry of divergent emotions flooded through her. He grinned as she flung her arms around his neck in an embrace. They hugged in silence for a few moments.

"Do you realise this is the first time we've met that you haven't tried to kill me?" quipped Stuart.

"Well the first time was your fault for not introducing yourself properly," countered Betty, "and the second time, I was, well, confused, to put it mildly."

"Yes, I should have left you tied up, then the misunderstanding wouldn't have mattered, and you wouldn't have been able to get away."

Betty's eyes widened.

"Well that's what my superiors are telling me - I was too much a gentleman to remove the ties around your hands and feet, but…"

"Has it got you into a lot of trouble then?" asked Betty.

"Well, it'll be OK now you've turned up, but it *was* pretty embarrassing."

"Oh, I'm sorry," said Betty sympathetically.

She ran her hands over the rather ordinary black winter jacket that he was wearing. "You don't look nearly so suave in this thing."

"Ah yes, that's another thing - what happened to my overcoat?"

"Oh, Stuart, you can't imagine how much comfort it gave me while I was confused and on the run. And I treasured it because it reminded me of you." Stuart looked surprised. "I felt very alone and vulnerable," she explained further. "Anyway, it's in the dry-cleaners round the corner. The bottom got a bit wet and grubby because it was so long on me. Actually it should be ready now - shall we collect it?"

"Strange how we always seem to be going to launderettes or dry-cleaners," remarked Stuart as Betty slipped her arm through his and led him off. "So where did you go?" he asked.

"I've spent the day going round the art museums - the 'Starkart Gallery' is particularly inspiring - modern art," she informed him.

"Ah. But no, I meant when you 'skipped out' from the van?" he insisted.

"Oh, well I think I would rather keep that to myself," she replied thoughtfully. "I was in a strange psychological state, I needed some space to regain my mental composure and ground myself again."

"Well OK, but I'm not sure Wheatley will be content with that answer," mused Stuart. "And how is your memory now," he continued. "How much can you remember?"

"At first, everything was very 'gappy', and then gradually everything before that evening came back, bit by bit. The last thing I remember that evening was George being irritating." Betty noted a strange look from Stuart. "I needed to sleep but he kept me awake - I think he was talking on the phone. But then there is a complete blank until I gradually woke in the van, and escaped. At least I *thought* I was escaping, then." Betty was pensive for a moment. "Tom said that you rescued me - tell me about that."

"Ah, top-secret MI6 mission - I can't share the details with you," muttered Stuart evasively. "White horse and stuff," he whispered playfully. "To be honest it was only possible because you had given that Constanța phone number to Tom earlier. We had a trace on its recent contacts, which included the kidnappers, and so I could follow their van. You don't want to know the grizzly details."

Betty smiled up at Stuart. They had reached the dry-cleaners, so the conversation stopped whilst Stuart's coat was retrieved. He carefully examined the hem all the way round the bottom, as the shop assistant looked anxious, bracing herself for a complaint. Betty, by contrast, liked the way Stuart took pride in his appearance. At length, he was satisfied, and he removed his black jacket and put on the overcoat, regaining the cultured appearance from his initial meeting with Betty. She hugged him to show approval and they left the shop.

"Where to now?" she asked.

"Well I could do with a meal," he suggested. "I had been waiting for you outside the hotel for a couple of hours."

"No problem, let's walk and find a restaurant. So where did you come from?" asked Betty.

"I have been searching for you the last couple of days. I scoured the area around where you left me with the out-of-action van, talked to the local police, visited a few local towns and asked around. I could find no trace. You went to ground very successfully - you'd make a good agent."

Betty laughed. "I think not," she retorted, "I was simply skating on my luck. Actually, I nearly died in the snow," she added pensively, remembering Otto the dog's vital intervention. Stuart looked concerned.

"Oh..." interjected Betty, suddenly anxious on remembering something else. "So it wasn't you who asked after me at the Dignitas clinic here in Zurich? Someone did."

"Tom called a local agent and asked him to do that - we knew there was a chance you would head there if you were able to," explained Stuart. Betty nodded with some relief at the explanation.

"So what will you do now?" asked Betty. "Do you have to go back to Austria - is that where you work?"

"Yes, but I have been told to see you onto a plane back to the

UK first," remarked Stuart.

"Sounds good to me," said Betty. "We get to spend some time together then."

"How about this place?" asked Stuart as they arrived at an interesting-looking café.

"OK. I want to choose my own food this time, though," quipped Betty, wagging a finger at him.

*   *   *

They sat and ate and talked for a long time. Betty was accustomed to not being able to disclose anything about the content of her work, so she easily accepted that Stuart could not reveal details about his either. Nevertheless, they found plenty to chat and deliberate about, and a bond of friendship grew quickly.

"You know," related Betty, "it's strange, when I came to Zurich I thought the progress of my medical condition was inevitable, *and* I thought I had accidentally killed you. So, I arrived in Zurich with the intention that an assisted suicide would put an end to both the guilt and the health decline. But it has turned out that both of those bad things were not true - it's as if I have been given a full reprieve on both counts - a chance to live again. And I learned to get back in touch with basics whilst I was on the run. It's as if everything has turned out perfectly." She was expecting Stuart to concur with a smile, but a troubled look passed over his face. "What is it, Stuart?" she asked with concern.

"Oh... well... nothing really."

"No. Tell me, Stuart. Don't keep things from me, please."

"Yes, I'm sorry, Tom was not sure we should tell you yet, whether you were ready to hear it. There is some bad news." Betty felt some panic. She focussed on Stuart's face. "George was killed in the kidnap."

"What... how..." Betty felt the grip of fear in her stomach.

"He was shot in the head by one of the kidnappers at the hospital."

"Oh, god... That's so unfair... not George..." Betty felt sick. "Excuse me."

Betty rushed to the ladies' restroom. She doubled over the toilet and vomited up most of the meal she had just eaten. "Oh George..." she muttered, tears in her eyes. Then the shock gave way to a strange angry heat in her face. She flushed the toilet and sat on it. She pulled out her phone and turned it on. She felt a fury that she had not ever experienced before. Her special app on the phone showed a green indicator - the equipment back at GCHQ was charged up and ready to use. She selected the callee GPS location mode, looked up the Constanţa number, and without any hesitation called it. There were two rings, then...

A man's guttural voice answered in Russian. "Да Слушаю?" Another indicator on her screen showed that the GPS location of the called phone had been successfully queried. She pressed the button. There was a sharp crack, and maybe a garbled cry over the phone. "That's for George," she whispered. Revenge accomplished, she turned the phone off again and returned it to her pocket. Then she cried long and hard.

After a couple of minutes, a waitress came in, sent by Stuart, to see if she was OK. She nodded and set about freshening herself up.

"I'm sorry, Stuart," she apologised on returning to their table, "that was a real shock. I feel wretched - there was me just saying everything had turned out perfectly. Can we walk by the river now - get some fresh air?" They left the café, linked arms and walked silently and sombrely - conversation had been displaced by Betty's sadness, and some guilt, since it was she who had suggested going to Austria.

∗   ∗   ∗

Stuart's phone rang. "Hi, Stuart, It's Tom. Listen, a warning, we might have some fresh trouble. We're still monitoring that Constanţa number. About half an hour ago there was a call made to it from a number we haven't seen before, but apparently made from central Zurich. The strange thing is it's logged as lasting only 3 seconds, and there have been no follow-on calls from either number. The Zurich number is now switched off so we can't track it. But it's a possibility they have an agent in Zurich - I can't imagine how they could have located her again, when even we were unable to find her until she checked-in with us. Anyway, take all precautions."

Stuart stiffened and quickly surveyed in all directions around where they were walking. "Sorry Betty, but I think we had better go back to your hotel, Tom has just indicated that there could be more trouble."

"What... Damn, I thought this nightmare was over." Betty

shivered; the fear was grabbing her again. "What did Tom say then?"

"Oh, It's probably nothing to worry about, but that Constanţa number took a call from a phone in Zurich half an hour ago."

Betty realised it had been her own call, and her fear abruptly dissipated. "Oh..." The tone in her voice was all wrong - it sounded like the relief that it actually was. "Yes, it's probably nothing," she added trying to sound matter-of-fact. But Stuart was very observant and had picked up the incongruous intonation.

"What?" He stopped walking and turned her to face him. "What did you mean by that? Do you know something?" Betty looked away and sighed. "What... Betty, did you make that call? Why? What's going on?" He pulled her more roughly to face him again.

"Well, yes, OK... I made that call... when I went to the ladies' room. I was so angry that they had killed George that I wanted to rant at that Constanţa bastard," she lied. "But when he answered I thought better of it and just ended the call. So no harm done."

"No harm done?" Stuart sounded incredulous. "MI6 have been having a bonanza tracing all the network of callers around that number. If you have spooked him, then that's finished. Shit, that's exactly why I was advised not to tell you about George yet - you get hysterical and do something crazy. Now I am in trouble for being too much the gentleman toward you again."

"Now, hang on a minute," protested Betty. "Let me remind you that the only reason you had that Constanţa number in the first place, was because I inveigled it out of the Austrian forensics guy. You admitted it yourself, all your heroics depended on having that number to facilitate tracking the kidnappers. Perhaps I'll just look after myself next time - you and the police are more trouble than you're worth." She pulled herself away from Stuart and strode off.

Then she turned to face him again. "Oh, and don't call me hysterical - you haven't begun to see what I am capable of yet."

Stuart was nonplussed for a moment. Then he made after her. "Wait, Betty, wait up... Tom said he hadn't seen the number before, so it can't be the one you were using at Villach. So presumably you have a new SIM card number?" Betty nodded curtly. "Have you made any other calls using it?"

Betty thought for a second. "No, I didn't call anyone, not even my mother, because I knew if I did, you lot would be able to trace me

141

again." Betty continued walking.

Stuart kept pace with her. "Exactly. So if we dispose of that SIM card now, then MI6 won't ever be able to link that Constanţa call to you; You won't get into trouble for making the call, and I won't get into trouble for making you hysterical."

Betty thumped him on the arm. "I was not hysterical, I was angry," she hissed.

"Whatever," protested Stuart. Betty narrowed her eyes, but deep down she knew that Stuart meant it humorously, and a trace of smile showed at the corner of her mouth.

"So?" continued Stuart.

"So what?"

"So are you going to surrender the SIM card to save both our souls?"

"I'll think about it."

Stuart sighed with impatience. "Betty…"

"OK, OK…" She pulled her phone out of a pocket, removed a glove and prised the back off with a fingernail. "Here…" She handed the SIM card to Stuart. He bent it in half and flicked it nonchalantly into the next trash bin they passed.

They walked on in silence for a while, in contrast to their lively conversation of earlier in the café.

"Are you OK? Are you still mad at me?" Stuart proffered at length.

Betty stopped and sighed, then leaned on the iron railings, looking out over the wide river. "I'm feeling a lot calmer now. I'm sorry Stuart - no, it's not you. I do really enjoy your company, but hearing about George has made me preoccupied. I feel partly responsible - it was me who suggested going on that skiing holiday together. It seems so unfair - he was just an academic spending a bit of time at GCHQ. I suppose you are used to conflict in your line of job, but my work colleague and me, we only ended up at GCHQ by chance really - it just happened that our research got a bit… hairy, so they took us under their wing. We are just not used to this type of… well, violent activity. It's confusing and unsettling, and in George's case, just plain tragic."

Stuart nodded and put his arm around Betty comfortingly. She responded by leaning into him. They remained in silence for a minute. "Would you like," suggested Stuart out-of-the-blue, "to go ice-skating?"

"Oh, no I don't think I feel like that right now."

"It's within walking distance," furthered Stuart, "and it is your last night here."

Betty took a deep breath. "Well... actually, OK, yes that would be fun. I suppose there's no point me moping. Which way is it?" Stuart pointed to a turning away from the river and they started to walk. "I know it sounds crazy, Stuart, but I'd really like to grab something to eat on the way - I'm afraid I sicked-up the café meal into the toilet, after I heard about George, so I'm hungry again now."

"No problem."

"And I need a new SIM card after you broke mine," she quipped.

"I think that will have to wait until tomorrow morning, the shops are shut for tonight," observed Stuart thoughtfully.

The rink was large and after a few circuits, as they gained their balance, they got warm, energetically tagging each other. Stuart was faster in a straight line but Betty was more adept on turns and manoeuvres. The fun continued for a while until Betty had an involuntary jerk on one of the bends, and went down spinning into the barrier. Stuart raced over, concerned.

"Are you OK?"

But Betty was laughing. "Yes, I've hurt my wrist a bit but... well, last week I was thinking I would only have to put up with these occasional twitches for a few more days, but now... they just make me realise that I need to get on that treatment program damn fast. I'll phone them straightaway, if I can get home tomorrow."

"You will," reassured Stuart. "Do you want to head back to the hotel?"

"No, let's do a few more circuits of the rink before we go, but not so fast this time."

Chapter 8
Homeward Bound

The next morning the passport arrived as promised, and after buying a new SIM card to make Betty's phone operational again, Stuart drove Betty out to the airport in his hire-car, where she booked onto a flight back to the UK. Betty felt elated to finally be going home and leaving behind the web of intrigue and danger that had blighted the last few days, though she was regretfully aware that George would not be going home, and she knew that she might face one or two awkward questions from MI5 about the fictitious laser-gun.

"So Stuart, I would really like it if you could come to visit me in the UK when you get some free time - is that possible?" asked Betty as they said their goodbyes at the departure gate.

Stuart nodded, "Yes I think that might be possible - I'll let you know."

"I won't give you my address because I'm sure you already know everything about me from my personnel file," quipped Betty making Stuart smile. "And I'm sorry," she continued, "if I have been a difficult client?" Stuart laughed. "But I have enjoyed your company." She hugged and kissed him before walking through the gate to the departure lounge. He watched her disappear into the crowd before phoning Tom Wheatley to tell him 'mission accomplished'. Then he booked himself onto a flight back to Vienna.

*   *   *

As Betty settled back during the flight she started to think through the issues she had to deal with when she got back. The experimental treatment program was straightforward - she knew which people to ring from the research paper and her own medical contacts. She just needed to get on with it as soon as possible.

The flight attendants began pushing the drinks trolley on its torturously slow crawl down the aircraft aisle.

Then there was the problem of how hard Tom Wheatley would push for explanations about the use of the fictitious laser weapon. She felt the best approach would be to say nothing, invoking the 'Official Secrets Act'. But she wasn't sure whether that might make the problem worse if Wheatley then discussed it with GCHQ - what was the relationship or hierarchy between them and MI5? However, if she *were* forced to explain in detail, she would then be able to assert that the Heiligenblut van offensive was carried out from, and by, a different timeline, so neither she nor her colleagues could be held responsible. In fact, that action might even have been sanctioned by MI5 in that timeline - there was no way to tell. And she could argue that it was her eventual deductions about that 'action from a different timeline' that had inspired and enabled her to develop the phone as a self-defence weapon. Then she could claim that she was not hiding the capability from GCHQ or MI5 - there had just been no time or opportunity, yet, to inform them of what she had discovered. That was all fine as long as Alex or George said, or had already said, nothing that would contradict her assertions about their research group previously knowing nothing about the offensive capability of the i-vector equipment. She must get to talk privately with Alex urgently. And... ah, but poor George could not say anything now... which led onto the final issue.

It would obviously be possible to use the equipment, targeting a particular event, to alter the timeline again to prevent George's death. Just zapping the two kidnappers before they got to the hospital would presumably achieve that. But... the previous attempt to change the timeline in her favour - by zapping the Heiligenblut kidnappers, had not resulted in a clean, quick change to the timeline - anything but. It had exposed the existence of the covert zapping technology, because of the unique nature of the burns it imposed, and it also had, somehow, allowed her to get ensnared in the aftermath. She shivered again as she remembered talking to Alex about her conjecture, or gut feeling, that time seemed to be conspiring to get events back to 'how they should be'. Alex had roundly rejected what she was saying as irrational - but it *had* happened - she *had* been eventually kidnapped. Although admittedly, that subsequent abduction had been thwarted. But, only by a combination of her guile with the Constanţa phone number and Stuart's skills. So, did that rescue invalidate her unsettling conjecture about the nature of time, or... might her true destiny still be unfulfilled... might she *still* yet be in for another abduction. The thought was chilling. Indeed she wondered, was it coincidence that George was shot in the *head* the day after he fell and injured his head? She shuddered at the image.

Just then, the drinks trolley was alongside, and the stewardess was asking what Betty wanted. She decided to put the fear out of her mind and get into celebration mode - she was, at last, going home, against all odds. She asked for two mini-bottles of champagne.

She gracefully sipped champagne from the inelegant plastic cup, remembering the time they had simulated rainfall in the lab by perforating a plastic cup with a pin, and filling the cup with water. She smiled, then drifted back to her reasoning. There was the still-unanswered question about altering a timeline - did it just create a new timeline, leaving the old timeline intact? If so, she would never see George again anyway, he was gone from this timeline forever. But then the issue of whether to change the timeline shouldn't be about *her* feelings... didn't George have a right to be resurrected into another timeline? Certainly, the zap offensive at Heiligenblut showed that others, presumably her colleagues, had decided that she, Betty, was worth saving - that it was valid to perhaps 'look after your own'. Or were there bigger issues feeding that decision - the fact that she would be tortured to reveal the i-vector secrets to hostile agents? Had the primacy of the GCHQ secret been the driving factor, rather than her well-being?

On the other hand, if there is only one timeline, and that gets changed, then George is back, but she would lose her memories of being with Greta, of visiting the Zurich Opera House - those things would never happen, would never have happened.

This all required a very long discussion with Alex - the ethical consideration of whether a change should be effected or not, and if so, how to do it neatly and cleanly, so that it wouldn't raise questions over implausible burn marks in autopsies, *if* there was such a way. And perhaps they could do experiments to conclusively establish whether a change did affect the extant timeline, or alternatively caused the generation of a new parallel timeline - though she couldn't quite envisage what that experiment might entail.

⁎　　⁎　　⁎

"Hello, Betty." Betty had forgotten that Tom Wheatley had said he would meet her at the airport. He recognised her easily, having studied her photographs, and although she had no idea what he would *look* like, she recognised his voice immediately - that reassuring tone of an older, wiser man. He adjusted his gold-rimmed spectacles and smiled at her, flashing a rather impressive ID card to her in a gesture that would preclude others from seeing it. "Welcome home, and it's good to meet you at last. I can't tell you how glad I am that you are finally back - there were times this past week when we were frantic with worry." It was actually difficult for Betty to imagine such a calm, confident man being frantic, but she smiled back and shook his hand in greeting. "My driver is outside, we'll take you home. You're travelling light?" he asked, looking at her single carrier bag.

"Well, you have my case, I believe, couriered from Villach?"

"Yes, indeed we do. We'll reunite you with it tomorrow."

There were obviously privileges that came with MI5 employment - the luxury car was parked right outside the main door on double-yellow lines. Wheatley courteously opened a door for her and then settled himself in by the opposite door. He slid open a panel in the partition separating them from the driver. "The Cheltenham address please, Parker," and closed the panel again.

Betty laughed. "Is his name really Parker?"

"Yes, why?" Wheatley looked genuinely puzzled.

"Oh, that was the name of Lady Penelope's chauffeur in 'Thunderbirds' - it's kind of archetypical. I must say I didn't expect to be picked-up by a limousine when you said you would meet me."

"Ah, well I can work while I am in the limousine, it's private. I hope you won't mind talking with me while we drive - I'd like to get the debriefing done immediately."

"Sure."

"So talking of name associations, do you know where the word 'limousine' originates from?"

"No."

"The shepherds in the French region of Limousin used to wear big, specially-shaped hoods to keep the rain off them." He was pulling a mobile phone out of his pocket as he spoke. "And the earliest cars that had a private section for the travellers, had no roof over the driver - he was left out in the weather. So, those chauffeurs also used to wear the same big hood as the shepherds in Limousin. Hence, the association and adoption of the name. Fortunately, these days, things are more comfortable, and Parker has a roof over his head. Excuse me a second." He spoke into the phone. "Ben, it's Tom. Yes, Miss Gosmore is with us - we are taking her home now." He returned the phone to his pocket, but pulled a recording device out of his briefcase, and placed it between them on the car seat.

The car was now picking up speed on open road and was remarkably smooth and quiet.

"So Betty, firstly I have to apologise on behalf of the UK security services that you have had to endure the experiences that you have. We failed to protect you, which we had a duty to do. Of course, our fundamental priority in a case like this is keeping our secrets secure, and indeed these were put at risk, but we do also place high value on the well-being of our government employees. As for the failings of the Austrian police protection, I made the judgement that you would be safe with them. I was wrong, and in retrospect, I should have put agents in to protect you. So again I am sorry."

Betty acknowledged the apology with a nod. "I understand."

"So we have already analysed your old phone. Invisible malicious software had been loaded into it that transmitted your location. The malware also recorded all your calls and texts and transmitted them to a third party internet mailbox. We are trying to identify to whom that mailbox belongs, but it almost certainly is linked with that Constanţa number of which you cleverly informed us. That number saved your life, by the way, since we were able to trace the recent callers to it, which included the kidnappers, and consequently we were able to track their phone and follow the abduction route until we could intercept. Anyway, that much we know. What we don't yet know is how the kidnappers were able to get that software onto your phone, or how they were able to identify you as a person with valuable secrets, though I have some theories. Now would you mind looking at these photographs of yourself - the ones that the Austrian police found amongst the possessions of the Heiligenblut kidnappers? We have blown them up." He drew out a set of A4 photographs from his briefcase and handed them to Betty. He switched on a light in the back of the car, and handed her a magnifying glass. "Just take your time and tell me any details you can see. We are particularly interested in places and dates."

Betty flicked through them quickly then went back to studying them one by one. "This third one is quite easy. I am just leaving the GCHQ annexe - you can see the door behind, and the security desk through that."

"OK, so for *them*, that identifies you as someone who works there. And we must presume that they already have identified that place as being 'of interest'." He sighed. "I do question the wisdom of putting special projects in separate buildings. Although it is also quite likely that they were tipped off by someone on the inside. Anyway, that is for us to investigate. Can you tell when that photo was taken?"

"Not really, it must be cold because I have a scarf on as well as a coat - actually, that coat is an old one, I haven't been wearing that *this* winter. So my guess would be *last* winter."

"Good. Try the other photos."

"Well, these two look similar - they could be the same day, same place, or they could be on other days. It's difficult to see from the small amount of background. Then this one is the photo I've already seen, and the final one looks similar - in both I'm wearing my new coat, I bought that about... the second week in September, so the photo has to be after then. And the little bit of background - Ah, there's more on the other picture." Betty used the magnifying glass to examine the detail. "It looks like a shop display with games and tablets. Ah! I know where this is. One day, when I was taking the things out of my bag for front-desk security check, I dropped my phone and the screen cracked. So, I took it into a phone repair shop in town - in Cheltenham, on my way home. It's in one of the little roads off the shopping area in High Street. Hang on a minute." She removed her new phone from her pocket and called up Google maps, zooming in on the shopping centre. "So, there it is, FastPhone, 14 Regent St. The buggers - they hacked my phone while they were repairing the screen," declared Betty angrily.

"And you may not be the only one. A clever ruse really - setting up near a security establishment, photographing and identifying their targets as people coming out of the high-security area, then getting occasional matches with their in-shop CCTV, so as to identify which phones to hack. Excellent deductions - thank you, Betty. Excuse me a minute" He pulled his own phone out of his pocket to make a call.

"Well, I won't be recommending *them* again," Betty declared.

Wheatley froze in his movement. "Again?"

"Yes, they were quite fast, I picked it up the following morning, and it was immaculately done, so I recommended it to my friend Emilia when she had a problem with her phone." Betty noticed the look of concern on Wheatley's face. "Oh, no it's OK, she doesn't work at GCHQ," laughed Betty.

"We'll check it anyway," remarked Wheatley, as he resumed making his call. "Hi, Ben, can you liaise with the police to raid 'FastPhone, 14 Regent St, Cheltenham' - it's the source of the Malware, and get a message sent round to all GCHQ personnel requesting that if anyone has used that shop they contact us urgently. Thanks."

Wheatley sighed. "Good. Now can you please fill me in on everything that happened after the kidnap? Where you were, and with whom, for all that time" Wheatley listened without interrupting as Betty recounted her gradual awakening from the sedative and the events that followed. She omitted to say anything about the zap that had been intended for the kidnappers but had instead damaged the driver's area of the van while Stuart had fortunately been getting food and coffee. And she omitted specifics about Greta's name and address. She also omitted any reference to her call to Constanța and the subsequent pact with Stuart about it. But she did include plenty of detail in an attempt to satisfy Wheatley who listened intently.

"Thank you, Betty. I appreciate your candour, and I am very well aware that this nearly ended in tragedy for you - thank goodness that dog found you." Betty nodded grimly. Indeed, at the time she had not been in a state of mind to appreciate the narrow escape from a snowy death. "So it would help us, just to dot the i's and cross the t's, so to speak, if you could give me the old woman's name and where the chalet was, so we can get confirmation from her?"

Betty shook her head. "I don't want to do that, Tom. She is an elderly woman living simply, on her own - I don't want her disturbed. Besides, I told her I had been kidnapped. So she would be alarmed at strangers calling and would not tell them anything, for my sake."

Wheatley nodded slowly. "OK. Now the other detail you said nothing about is how you did, what you did, to Stuart's van?"

Betty sighed. She had already extracted one concession from Wheatley on Greta's privacy. She pointed down at the recording device, and Wheatley acknowledged her gesture by switching it off. "You see Tom, even if I had some sort of covert offensive capability - which I neither confirm nor deny, I am subject to the Official Secrets Act, and I would be able to say nothing about it. I would also add that you can clearly see that the alleged use of any such capability has only happened as an act of self-defence, and in situations which resulted from lack of competence by the UK security umbrella. So I think it would be extremely unfair to pressure me on this point."

Wheatley took a deep breath and thought for a moment. "I take your point Betty, and I assume the same goes for the three kidnapper deaths?"

"Three?" echoed Betty interrogatively, not understanding.

"Oh, I'm sorry, yes, I guess you won't remember. Apart from the two who were despatched in the Heiligenblut van crash, there was one killed in similar fashion at the hospital during the kidnap."

"Oh!" exclaimed Betty, nonplussed for a moment. She tried to compute what difference, if any, that made. "Well I know nothing about that - Stuart didn't tell me, though he did tell me about George getting shot."

"You see," said Wheatley in explanation, "the problem is that agents being killed with extremely unorthodox burn marks is likely to attract the attention of foreign powers, and we may, as a result, get additional undesirable efforts by them to acquire our secrets."

"Yes, Tom, I am acutely aware of that. It is regrettable that it ever happened, but I repeat that the alternative was me being tortured by enemy agents, which I can assure you, would result in the *immediate* revealing of secrets."

"You are right of course. At least this way we have the opportunity to try to sweep the autopsies under the table. The Austrian police are so embarrassed about losing you from their so-called protection that I am able to call in favours, especially as all three dead men are proven to be engaged in criminal abduction. As far as I know, the nature of their deaths has not travelled beyond the pathologist and the few police involved." The additional zap in Constanţa flashed into Betty's mind as an embarrassing complication - perhaps she had been too hasty? "Meanwhile, this end," continued Wheatley, "we are checking a lot of GCHQ personnel phones, to identify any further security breaches. We will probably close the annexe and house your team elsewhere. We may give you a new identity. And so on. And then, of course, we will be investigating how the special status of your annexe came to be leaked to hostile agents - was it a loose tongue, or a deliberate, or coerced, act of betrayal?

"Anyway," Wheatley shifted his position in the seat, "let's leave that subject now. Tell me about your amnesia. What is the last thing you can remember? And do you feel OK now?" He switched the recording device back on, and listened as Betty, now on more comfortable ground, related the edges of the missing part of her memory of the kidnap evening. It was, however, emotionally difficult remembering and recounting the final half-hour of her memory - the irritation with George she had felt, now knowing that he died only minutes after that.

"That sounds," concluded Wheatley, "like a fairly typical experience under that drug. We have several accounts now of its effects - it seems to prevent the formation of memories from shortly before its administration until several hours afterwards, and those memories are never recovered. But the good news is that it seems to have no long-term side-effects. We can take you to a hospital now to get you checked out, if you like, but I expect you would rather get back home this evening?"

"Actually I would really like to be dropped off at my colleague, Alex's, home - I very much want to spend some time with him after everything that's happened."

"Ah yes, Alex, lovely fellow, I met him this afternoon. We have already checked his phone - it was fine - no malware - so his address is perfectly safe. We may want to find you a new home, though."

"What? No, I love my home - I don't want to move," protested Betty.

Wheatley laughed. "OK, we'll talk about it tomorrow. I will be around GCHQ for at least the next few days while we are investigating the security breach. And don't hesitate to call me on the phone if you want me for anything."

*   *   *

A while later, Wheatley's limousine pulled up outside Alex's house. Betty thanked Wheatley, shaking his hand, and then walked up to Alex's front door with her single carrier bag. It was Petra that first greeted her with a big hug, as Alex then joined in and the kids danced around their feet. Wheatley watched the endearing scene for a moment from the car window before instructing his driver to return them to their hotel.

The questions were kept necessarily low-key whilst the kids were got ready for bed, and then Betty read them a goodnight story, while downstairs a meal was cooked for the grownups. Over supper, Betty recounted her story, at least as much as she could in front of Petra who was not party to the covert technology. They were all very aware of George's absence, especially since he and they had shared a similar meal together only two weeks before. Petra asked a few questions to try to understand why the Austrian police had persisted in detaining Betty even after they understood her identity. However, when she realised that Betty was not free to explain it all to her, she generously suggested that Alex take Betty out for a celebratory drink, knowing that the two of them needed to catch up on matters outside her remit.

In fact, Alex first drove them out to 'their hill' in a field outside the city, which was where they always retired to, if they needed to discuss anything in absolute privacy. It was a cold evening, but fortunately not wet, so as usual, they left their coats in the car, donning blankets - a precaution against the possibility of bugging-devices in coats, and trudged up to the crest of the hill where they sat to talk. Betty went through each of the issues that she had ruminated on during the flight, whilst Alex listened.

"Yes, I've been wondering about many of the same things myself," began Alex in reply. "It does seem that those offensive zaps are likely to attract too much attention of the sort we don't want. I suppose if that Heiligenblut zap had been aimed at exploding the van's fuel tank, instead of hitting the drivers, then that might not have raised awkward questions. But, importantly, if the fuel tank had been successfully targeted, then we would not have known about the kidnap attempts or the security problems at all, because you would have just travelled onto Zurich without incident. So, that would simply mean that we would be vulnerable again, in the future. I suppose ideally we would both hit the fuel tank, and also send a message to the new timeline, explaining the security problems - if we could find a way of doing that.

Perhaps we should just resist the temptation to use any further zaps, particularly if you think the Austrian police can successfully bury the evidence of what has happened so far, then we start with an essentially clean sheet as of now. There are more subtle ways of changing the course of events, such as sending a message back to our previous selves - not that we have an organised way of doing that as of yet."

They were interrupted by a call coming through on Alex's phone. "Hi, Alex. Sorry to bother you but there seems to be something wrong with the equipment." It was Harriet who had resumed military surveillance night shifts using the i-vector equipment in the lab. "The first picture I did was kind of fuzzy, so I repeated it, but now I am getting completely blank pictures. It's just not working," she concluded. Alex smiled at the very non-technical description.

"Right. Yes, it does sound like there is a fault. Mmm... there's not anything I can do about it tonight, I am out for a drink with Betty."

"Oh, is she back? That's great. Hey, perhaps I'll just come and join you guys then."

"Ah, OK," laughed Alex. "We'll meet you in the Sandford Park Alehouse."

Betty looked at Alex quizzically.

"Harriet," Alex explained. "The machine is not working. So, she's meeting us for a drink. Anyway, I think it's best we take time to think these issues through thoroughly, there's no rush to fix anything immediately. Not that we could anyhow, if the equipment is not working."

Betty was disappointed at the interruption. She had been hoping to clarify some of the questions, and had wanted to get round to telling Alex about the revenge zap she had actioned against the hostile agent in Constanţa. She had been feeling increasingly regretful about having acted in anger and haste - exposing the technology again with those inexplicable burns, but she was also concerned about whether it might have caused collateral injury to anyone close by. Of course, she could always retrospectively neutralise the zap with an anti-zap - all the data and coordinates to calculate that would be stored in the computers controlling the equipment. So, the plan forming in her head was to do some retrospective surveillance of the scene immediately after the zap at Constanţa before deciding whether or not to erase her impetuous act.

*   *   *

SATURDAY 7th January

Betty spent some time messaging and calling medical contacts to try to arrange getting into the Huntington's experimental treatment trial, before she headed into the lab. Alex had already been there for a couple of hours, trying to understand what had gone wrong with the machinery, to no avail, by the time Betty arrived. He frustratedly started explaining what he was seeing on the screen when he tried to run it.

"Whoa, first things first," declared Betty, switching on the coffee machine, and then putting a reassuring hand on his shoulder. "Have you run the diagnostic suite?"

"What diagnostic suite?"

"I wrote all the diagnostic software whilst we were installing the equipment, remember?" explained Betty.

"Oh, I thought that was all ad hoc," retorted Alex.

"Well it *was* ad hoc at the time, but I consolidated it all into a diagnostic program afterwards, otherwise it would just get wasted." Betty went over to one of the other computer screens and started up her analysis software. "Right, give it a few minutes, and we'll see what comes up." She reverted to the coffee machine, which was making encouraging noises.

At that moment the door opened and Tom Wheatley appeared. "Good morning Betty… Alex."

"Oh, Hi Tom, you're working the weekend too, are you?" Betty greeted him.

"Yes, we need to push on with investigating the initial security breach, and we've raided that 'FastPhone' shop that you pointed us to, and made some arrests. Our experts are combing through their equipment right now. But I also had some more bad news last night." He did look less relaxed than when Betty had been with him the previous day. "I'm sorry to tell you that Kelvin has gone missing."

Alex and Betty looked at each other blankly. "Kelvin? Who's Kelvin?"

"Oh, I assumed you would know him - one of the lads who works in the next lab along - BF5?" supplied Wheatley.

"Ah, yes, we're not allowed to socialise with the other groups here, so we have no idea what they are working on, but I think I do know the lads by sight," explained Alex.

"Well it seems he went to Poland a few days ago," explained Wheatley, "to attend a scientific conference on Nuclear physics, and has just disappeared. One of my team has confirmed that there is a payment on his credit card account late last year to that 'FastPhone' outfit - so it looks very much like he has suffered an abduction in similar fashion to the way yours was organised, Betty."

Betty's hand went to her mouth. "Oh no, poor guy."

"The only silver lining," continued Wheatley, "is that his team have apparently not come up with any innovative science or technology, so when the information is extracted from him, the hostile agents may conclude that this place is not worth any further effort. Unless, of course, he tells them that he has no idea what you other guys are working on," Wheatley added thoughtfully. "Anyway, the phones of everyone else working in the annexe, have been checked now, so if he is the only one we lose, then that's not so bad an outcome."

"It seems a bit harsh to write him off like that," berated Betty. "Haven't you any idea where he might be?"

"No. I fully expect that it is the Constanţa connection again," added Wheatley, "we have a couple of our agents digging around to see if we can pinpoint their agent there."

"I find it difficult to believe that his work is of no innovative value," interjected Alex. "There must have been some good reason why their project ended up here in GCHQ. Could I perhaps read through their laboratory logbooks and give an opinion?" Betty looked at Alex in surprise.

Wheatley thought about the suggestion for a moment. "Actually a second opinion from another nuclear physicist, such as yourself, would be a good idea since there is so much potentially at stake. I will try to arrange for that. Anyway, I'll let you get on - I gather you've got a broken machine to fix." He left, looking preoccupied.

*   *   *

"So what was that offer of a second opinion about, Alex?"

"Well it certainly won't do him, Kelvin, any harm to talk up his importance, and also I am genuinely concerned." Alex paused thoughtfully. "And I suppose - what's that phrase that Bowen uses? - I am consumed by curiosity," he laughed.

Betty tutted. "Well I suppose there's no other way we can help is there?" she looked at Alex knowingly - they both realised that to make a timeline intervention they would need to know Kelvin's exact location, at an appropriate point in time. But to establish that using surveillance on him with pictures from the equipment, would require at least a reasonable starting point, and they had no idea where to begin. Of course, such issues could not be discussed in the lab, anyway, in case they were being monitored.

Betty turned back to her computer screen whilst taking sips of coffee. She scrolled through the masses of diagnostic data on the screen. "It's the septum magnets, they're powered on, but the magnetic field is misaligned," she stated matter-of-factly.

Alex opened his mouth to say something, then closed it again. He walked through into the equipment room and picked up his screwdriver.

Betty laughed. "It's good to have you back, Betty!" she suggested to the otherwise empty room. She put her feet up on the desk and concentrated on enjoying the rest of her coffee.

∗ ∗ ∗

About a half hour later Alex emerged looking pleased with himself. "Can you try the diagnostics again please, Betty," he requested. "I found one of the septum magnet housings had worked loose - probably from the vibrations. I've tightened it up again. It should be OK now." A re-run of the diagnostics indeed showed that the problem had disappeared.

"Well done, Alex. Here is your reward." Betty handed Alex a small pile of laboratory logbooks from Kelvin's lab which Tom Wheatley had dropped in whilst Alex had been busy with the equipment. She smiled to see his eyes light up as he eagerly delved into the pages and quickly became engrossed.

Since he was now preoccupied, and seemed oblivious to what she was doing, Betty decided to set up the equipment to take a retrospective picture of the scene at Constanţa a couple of seconds after she had actioned that overly hasty zap the evening before last. Some hard evidence would be better than not knowing, and would at least be a start in determining whether or not she needed to nullify that zap. She took the erstwhile coordinates of the Constanţa phone and backed them off a metre or two in a direction that would give a view of the holder of the phone. Betty started the preparation of a particle cloud. It would be a half-hour wait. She made some more coffee and found some bits to do on the computer. At length, Alex's silent intensity tried her patience.

"So what are the lads next door working on?" asked Betty.

"Oh, er... the quantum Zeno effect," muttered Alex without looking up.

"What, 'Zeno', as in 'that annoying ancient Greek philosopher who didn't understand calculus'?" asked Betty dismissively.

"Er, well the effect is also known as 'Turing's paradox' if you prefer that," stated Alex scathingly. "Anyway Zeno lived 2,000 years before calculus was invented, so you can't hold ignorance against him."

"I would contend that it's a paradox that a paradox could be named after both Zeno *and* Turing."

Alex said nothing and kept on reading. Betty debated in her mind whether to google the effect to read about it, or get Alex to explain it to her. She decided on the latter.

"Come on Alex, explain the effect to me, and what they are using it for?"

"Oh, OK," sighed Alex resignedly, leaning back in his chair. "So, it's about the speed at which quantum transitions happen. Let's take a specific example of some radioactive material. It will naturally decay according to its average half-life. And each atom is in a quantum superposition of decayed and not-decayed as we wait for the decays to happen. But if photons of a suitable wavelength are pulsed at the nuclei, then the atoms are forced out of their superposition of decayed and not-decayed states - forced to fall back into one or other of those definite states. And if that is done after a short time, then the atom is overwhelmingly likely to fall into the not-decayed state, because probabilities are proportional to squared amplitudes, whereas…"

"…Whereas amplitudes behave linearly," supplied Betty, beginning to get the thrust of the explanation.

"Right," confirmed Alex. "So if we keep probing the atoms with appropriate pulses, then they keep falling back into the non-decayed state, and then have to start their superposition towards decay over again. So this repeated probing leads to the atoms being prevented from decaying. That means you have slowed down or even stopped the radio-active decay, you have increased the half-life, and that's what is called the Quantum Zeno effect."

"Ah, so they named it after Zeno because he invented those silly paradoxes about time and progression."

"Exactly - Achilles and the Tortoise."

"Then I still think they gave too much credit to Zeno."

Alex laughed. "Yes, the effect was actually predicted by von Neumann and Alan Turing, but someone later likened it to Zeno's paradox and the name stuck. Anyway, a few years ago it was found that by using a different type of pulse, one could *speed up* the quantum transitions - and so that's called the Quantum *anti*-Zeno effect."

So what is the GCHQ interest - what are they hoping to do with it?" asked Betty.

"Well, I'm only part way through the first logbook," protested Alex. "I don't know yet. But if you can speed up radioactive decay you could use lower-grade fissionable material in a nuclear power station, and get more out of it, or you might even be able to make a nuclear weapon explode prematurely. And if you could slow down fission you might be able to stop a nuclear weapon from going off at all. But I'm speculating, and it's not confined to just radioactivity - the effect works on any superposition of quantum states. Of course, the pulses have to be of an exactly appropriate frequency, and they would have to be able to penetrate any material surrounding the atom - those seem to be the difficult areas from my reading so far."

At that moment, there was a knock on the door and Wheatley reappeared. In contrast to earlier in the day when he had clearly looked worried, his avuncular air had now returned and he looked relaxed. "Hello again you two," he started, "I thought you would like to hear the good news - Kelvin has re-surfaced - he turned up at that scientific conference hotel again late last night, but we only just found out." Betty noticed Alex shift his position to hide the pile of logbooks in case Wheatley remembered them, judged Alex's opinion to be unnecessary now, and decided to take them away.

"I've had a briefing," continued Wheatley, "from my agent who is looking after Kelvin at the moment, and it's quite a strange tale. Kelvin says he *was* abducted - he thought he was getting into a taxi, but was driven off in what he thought was the wrong direction. Then he can't remember much at all until he woke up in the back of a van feeling very hungry, and with his hands and legs tied. After a long, uncomfortable ride, he was eventually taken out of the van by two men, who freed his legs so they could walk him along a quayside and onto a large motor yacht, where they sat him down on a chair inside the cabin. There was another man in the cabin, whom he thinks was the boss, because that man checked Kelvin's face against a photo and checked Kelvin's passport, before counting out a pile of Euro notes for each of the two abductors. Then the boss's phone rang, he answered it, and - this is where it gets really bizarre. Kelvin says there was a sudden explosion that knocked the boss man down, the two abductors jumped up looking scared, grabbed their money and ran out, leaving Kelvin there, with the boss on the floor, whom Kelvin thinks was dead, though he didn't want to check. Kelvin says he thought he was being rescued so he just sat there for a couple of minutes waiting. Then when he realised no one was coming, he stood up, shuffled to the galley and found a knife that he worked with to cut the tie around his hands. He realised they had taken his phone and wallet, so, he says he grabbed some food out of the fridge as he was starving hungry, took the rest of the pile of Euro notes and his passport, and just walked off the boat. He had no idea where he was, so he got well away from the boat, found a hotel and holed up for the night. He deduced from the 'Welcome pack' in the hotel room that he was in Constanţa, Romania. Then the next morning he asked the hotel reception people the way to the airport - he said they spoke surprisingly good English. And so, he found the bus to Bucharest airport, and from there flew back to Poland and eventually, very late last night, arrived back at the conference hotel.

"I'm relieved of course, but I do wish he had notified us sooner - he hadn't realised that we were aware of his abduction and were trying to find him. But the most extraordinary aspect of the story is the explosion, as he described it, which took out the agent in Constanţa at just the right time. When I pressed him, he said it was more like a flash of lightning - no smoke or anything. Maybe reminiscent of the way your kidnappers at Heiligenblut were fortuitously and mysteriously killed, isn't it Betty? - I don't suppose I will get any better an explanation out of *him* than I did from you. Unless we really do have guardian angels looking after you GCHQ people!"

"So when *was* the incident in the cabin of the boat?" asked Betty.

"Oh, well… that would have been the evening before last - Thursday, the 5th. Why?"

"Just trying to place it," said Betty.

"Well, let's think, that's the evening you were with Stuart in Zurich, isn't it, so you're not a suspect in this one," laughed Wheatley.

Betty immediately regretted asking - Wheatley was only a whisker away from remembering and associating the brief, monitored phone call from Zurich to Constanţa, with the events in the cabin.

"Oh well," Wheatley looked at his watch, " I need to get off to the airport now to meet Kelvin and de-brief him." He left with a smile on his face.

"Another timeline change," muttered Alex. "We really are being looked after. But I wonder how they established the coordinates to do it - it must have been a huge surveillance task."

"Well..." Betty hesitated.

"Well what?"

"Oh, nothing." Betty decided not to explain her phone-call coordinate method, or the fact that it had in reality been her own action, and had not been a timeline change. Not to explain it at the moment anyway. Not in the lab. Alex had already returned his attention to the logbooks, and she could see that he would be preoccupied for the rest of the day. Though she did not like having secrets from Alex - she needed someone that she could share everything with.

Betty turned back to the computer and used the keyboard to call up, onto her screen, the picture that had been processing for the last half hour. The black and white image scrolled into view: A man lay sprawled face down on the floor, two agitated burly men making for the door, a frightened geeky-looking youth sitting on a chair watching the scene unfold. She deleted the picture. There was no question of nullifying that zap now.

"OK, Alex I ran a test picture," she stated innocently, "the equipment is all fine again for Harriet's night shift. I'm off home now."

"Oh, OK Betty, Thanks. See you Monday morning?" Alex was courteous enough to raise his head from the logbooks to give Betty a smile before she departed.

*   *   *

Betty walked home. And as she walked, she began to feel an ache. She was just beginning to miss George acutely. Until now, events had always kept her busy, distracting her from actually feeling the loss of him, not giving her time to contemplate his absence. Indeed, there had always been the possibility of making a timeline change so that he would not die. But knowing what she now knew, that could not be done - the events saving Kelvin depended directly on her angry reaction upon learning that George had been killed. Any timeline change that saved George would put Kelvin back in jeopardy.

She decided to make a trip back to the place where she had first got close to George - the riverside seat and wooden dog statue that they had visited together. Where she had played an elaborate prank on him and they had kissed for the first time. It was a beautiful spot and there she could quietly pay tribute to his memory.

She retraced the drive through beautiful countryside across the Wye valley, eventually arriving in Hereford, and parked in the small car park near the river, as she had done with him on that occasion before. Was it really only two months ago? So much had happened in that time. Then alone she walked slowly along the towpath to find the spot. But when she arrived there she was horrified to see that the treasured rustic wooden seat had been trashed with red graffiti, and so had the dog. She slumped down onto the seat and cried bitterly for a long time.

*   *   *

Finally, all cried out, she rose and went back to the car. Now it was time to visit her mother. Another half-hour drive and she was pulling up on the gravel drive outside the family home that she knew and loved so well. Betty had discussed her medical condition with her mother after Christmas, just two weeks previously. Her mother, though devastated, had been fully supportive of Betty's decision to go for an assisted suicide, having lived through the years of torment with Betty's father as he declined. In fact, she had been expecting the sad news of Betty's assisted death to come any day now. At the revelation that there was now a chance for Betty to live a full and long life, her joy, therefore, was palpable, and they hugged long and hard, before Betty sat down to tell her the full story of the extraordinary week she had just lived through. Betty's mother basked in the joy of having a child returned, back from the brink of death. And Betty finally felt safe.

ABOUT THE AUTHOR

Allan Brewer had a career in writing software before researching in computational biochemistry for a PhD. Some of his erstwhile colleagues may reflect he will be more suited to science *fiction* than science! He is now retired in Bristol, caring for his granddaughter and walking her dog.

If you have enjoyed reading this book please write a **review** on its Amazon page - even just a sentence will do - reviews are the lifeblood of an author.

If you would like to be notified of further novels by this author, or to contact the author, please email to **AllanBrewerBooks@gmail.com**

Or visit the author's website **AllanBrewer.Wordpress.com** for a blog on cherry-picked real science.

The i-Vector Series

#1 Schrödinger's Dog

#2 The Constanţa Connection

Made in the USA
Lexington, KY
14 December 2019